A House by the River

Also by Sid Smith

SOMETHING LIKE A HOUSE

SID SMITH

A House by the River

PICADOR

First published 2003 by Picador
an imprint of Pan Macmillan Ltd
Pan Macmillan, 20 New Wharf Road, London N1 9RR
Basingstoke and Oxford
Associated companies throughout the world
www.panmacmillan.com

ISBN 0 330 48123 1 HB
ISBN 0 330 41234 5 PB

1 3 5 7 9 8 6 4 2

A CIP catalogue record for this book is available from
the British Library.

Typeset by SetSystems Ltd, Saffron Walden, Essex
Printed and bound in Great Britain by
Mackays of Chatham plc, Chatham, Kent

Acknowledgements

I am grateful to Erik Mueggler for permission to use his translation of the exorcism chant featured on pages 116–20 of this work. The chant is taken from pages 32–7 and 203–35 of Dr Mueggler's *The Age of Wild Ghosts* (University of California Press, 2001).

The foreigners are many,
but if we all spit once they will drown

Anti-Western leaflet, China, 1900

PROLOGUE

The river runs for a thousand miles across south China. It rises in the outposts of the Himalayas and struggles for half its length among the rapids and gorges of the foothills. Hundreds of miles from the source it's still swift and cold where it passes a pebble beach.

Downstream the river escapes the hills. It slows in China's subtropical plains and merges with the ocean in the great estuary which borders Canton and Hong Kong. Here at the beach, though, its brown back is lumpy as rope and foams over upjutting rocks.

In the early years of the twentieth century, two Westerners came to the beach. Later, one of them sank into the river. He began to drown, but couldn't move because he was wounded. He willed himself up towards the light.

But he saw that the gods of China were stirring. They knew him for one of their own, and rose from the dark like crocodiles.

In the beginning, though, the beach was home to the fisher folk. They came from the lowlands, where the river is warm and shows a man's reflection, but had spread upstream through the generations until the river grew talkative, then bared its teeth around the rocks of the upland rapids. At last the current was too swift for boats, so the fisher folk came to the pebble beach on foot.

At first they only camped here, sleeping beside their lines for a summer month or two. But the beach lay in a great bend where the river was turned by a mountain, and they saw how the river slowed as it turned, growing wide and shallow. On the far bank, the mountain was undermined and its scree slid into the water. On this side, though, in the crook of the bend, the current slackened and left a crescent of white pebbles.

The fisher folk brought boats from their settlements downstream, dragging them on bamboo ropes against the current until they came to the quiet waters off the beach. While they fished, an old man stayed on the beach, turning the catch on drying racks, covering it during the thrashing summer storms and chasing away foxes and river birds. He buried their refuse in the gritty soil beside the beach and grew a few vegetables.

The land is limestone, which submits to water, so the valley sides are steep. Above the old man's garden the slope climbed swiftly to a great ridge, restless with sliding stones, the first arm of the mountains.

Tribespeople watched from this ridge. They were jealous of the boats, made of hardwood from downstream, and decided they were being robbed of fish they couldn't catch. Each winter they took anything the fisher folk left, even the fertilized earth, which steamed in the cold air and seethed with insects as they dug. One summer they painted their faces and raided the drying racks, stealing half the catch while the old man fled into the shallows and the fisher folk watched in silence from the river.

Next season the fisher folk camped off the far bank, sleeping in their boats tethered to half-submerged boulders, drying their fish on poles wedged into the grey scree, in terror of the rocks which tumbled from above.

The old man took charge and a trade began. The tribes acquired fish in exchange for game or for the crops they raised around their own summer camps, though the barter was made with grunts and mime and much suspicion.

The fisher folk returned to the beach and raised their improbable platforms, twice as tall as a man, which swayed above the shallows on driftwood poles as thin as a wrist. There was a floor of matting, a mat roof, and one mat wall that was moved to face the wind but taken down when the wind grew too strong, lest the whole trembling contraption should founder.

The fisher folk still slept in their boats, which were more precious than any dwelling, but now stayed at the beach through the winter, when snow in the mountains ceased to melt and there was less water to hide the fish. The fangs of half-submerged rocks became more numerous, but the water was so tame that even the tribes took to the shallows in their clumsy rafts, though they disliked the river, which crossed their land like a foreign army and was too cold to touch. The fisher folk, too, had lost their downstream affection for the river, and forgot how to swim.

But the river still took their dead: the old man was launched into the water in a fishskin cap, his wrists and ankles tied, his mouth sewn shut around his one treasure, a silver hook which would pay the fish god for passage to the underworld, or (some said) would convince the god that he was only a dead fish.

The fisher folk houses moved up the beach, acquiring thatched walls and roofs, and crouching on shorter, stronger poles. Women appeared around the houses and were watched by the tribes, who had ceased to resent the fisher folk, only bad-tempered old men recalling that the beach had once been theirs.

The fisher folk had caught all the fish in the shallows off the beach, dipping their bamboo scoops into the slick water or casting their nets, so they moved into midstream, which was too fast for nets and scoops, except perhaps during the winter drought. Instead they grew adept with hooks and occasionally spears.

The midstream fish were big from fighting the current. A man might catch nothing for days but when he trapped a midstream fish, dragging it to the shallows then leaping into the water to club it to death like a man, he could eat for a week. Downstream, fisher folk honoured the river for its muddy fecundity, because the fish were anonymous and unending. But here the great clean fish had to be beaten one by one, and the fisher folk shouted as each was wrestled ashore, strong as a leg. They grew contemptuous of their cousins downstream, who had to boil their drinking water and could hold a rod in each hand because the fish were small: if they were big, they seemed in recollection to have watery flesh or be diseased.

The fisher folk explored upstream. They took a tribal path along the narrowing gorge, wary of tigers and the poison darts of the tribesmen, launching their fishing lines from tiny beaches, or dropping them into mist from the walls of thunderous ravines, or balancing over slimy boulders to drift them into deep pools at the foot of rapids.

Young men went furthest. A few climbed to the high mountains and saw the river issue from the womb of a grey dragon. But all of them saw the monastery which stood among its graves in a side valley. Some learnt that they were reincarnations of dead monks and stayed there for ever, becoming will-less as water, finding themselves through obedience as water does. But the rest came back to the pebble beach because at last even young men cease to resent their parents.

During China's troubles the Emperor's grip loosened on the outposts and the river people almost forgot him, absorbed in their struggles with the river and each other. In times of peace his influence was renewed. Then tax collectors raised their pavilions on the beach, though the proceeds were disappointing: the fisher folk were no trouble, having known the land tax downstream, but the tribes lifted their mat houses and moved to other streams in other valleys.

But taxation meant protection, so the Yi people had

talks with the collectors. The region had been too troubled for farming, but assurances were made and an opium plantation appeared in the valley next to the beach.

This valley lay behind the great ridge above the beach. It had its own stream, fed by reliable springs, whose water grew muddy in irrigation channels among the poppies, at last entering the river downstream from the beach. Opium boats came, hauled by gangs of coolies, and it was the highest port on the river. The wealth of the Yi brought traders, who spread their goods on blankets, then on stalls, and the plantation was called Market Village.

The fisher folk sold their fish there, but felt subdued among the strange tribals from the hills, the bright clothes of the plantation slaves, and the wealth of the Yi planters, who had silver necklaces and strong houses, although the houses were on the ground where animals and dirt could come in. On their way to market, the young men of the fisher folk bathed in the icy river to remove the shameful smell of fish, and later sang in the moonlight as they staggered home drunk over the steep ridge, which they called the Hog – an auspicious animal to which it bore no resemblance.

The Yi plantation required a permanent tax collector. Two wooden houses, brought in sections from downriver, appeared on the slope above the fisher folk village. One was reserved for official visitors, and the second, higher up the slope, sheltered generations of collectors from the summer rains, though not from the stink of fish.

Next door, Imperial soldiers grumbled in a shed with no windows and an earth floor.

One collector was called Yue Fat. On a warm day in spring, relaxing on his veranda, he opened a package of official mail. He was startled to read that the pebble beach would be home to two white people.

1

John Gerrard knew nowhere but China. His parents, though, came from Sacramento, where his father had been a bank clerk and lay preacher.

The Chinese of California couldn't vote, own land, testify in court against a white person, or be buried in white cemeteries. They couldn't work for the State, nor send their children to public schools. At Marysville their houses were confined to floodland near the Yuba River, so in 1880 they raised a temple to Bok Kai, the god who brings rain yet averts floods. John's father was aggrieved: he preached nervously in the temple yard, but was grinned at.

He joined a Baptist mission to the poor, treading wooden ghettos where police and firemen did not go. The Chinese smiled and ate the Christian rice, but were seen later at their temples. Nevertheless he dreamt of a great harvest in the Orient.

'A fifth of humanity!' he said, though his wife frowned and turned away. 'A fifth!'

He approached the Holy Word Mission and was shown its library. He read of China's cruelties, its luxury and need, and how this oldest of nations knelt to devils and the dead. He learnt that the Papists were there.

His job at the bank was a treadmill of pettiness, and

he saw the glory of bringing China under the bright wings of the Lord. He grew a little red moustache, pale as a soup stain, and booked a passage with his outraged wife.

Off the coast of Alaska he was taken ill. As he rolled in a fever, Mrs Gerrard left the sick-room stench to pick her way among the coolies. How they distrusted each other, crouched like dogs over their unvarying possessions – a fan and umbrella, a straw mat, a red blanket, and a box with a curved lid which held their American savings and was at night their pillow.

The whites avoided her because she was only a missionary's wife, so she leant on the rail pretending to watch a smoking volcano among the icy mountains. Instead, though, she stored the ugliest images of the heathens, telling her husband how they huddled in a corner to smoke opium and gamble and how they had doubtless supplied the fever which gripped him. He said that they were ignorant of the Lord and therefore innocent: she had seen their sagging loincloths, though, and disagreed.

She ceased to argue with him, since her victory seemed assured: he had worsened during a storm in the Japan Sea, which he didn't notice among his restless fevers, and was committed to the deep two days out from Nagasaki.

On the quay at Hong Kong the new widow said, 'I want to go home.' The welcoming party – two ladies of the Mission with a bunch of flowers – was silenced, but marshalled arguments on the ferry to Canton. She was told of the great work to be done in China, the difficulty of booking a ship, and the delays in releasing Mission funds: but she noticed only the locked gates in the stairwells, which guarded against pirates among the passengers.

In the Mission building in Canton, her delicate condition became obvious and the ladies more insistent. Now she raged against China. She stayed indoors to avoid its clamour, but couldn't escape the flies in her tea and the flying ants in her food. Her boots grew mouldy and moth larvae writhed in her clothes. She ate dinner with her feet in paper bags to keep off biting insects. Towards the end of her term even these horrors were surpassed: she discovered the hell of pregnancy in a Cantonese midsummer.

She would not accept a native doctor, although the Mission assured her that Dr Mo was the most thoughtful Chinese in the city, and his wife's sister a Christian, though sadly Romish. Instead John's birth was attended by the only women at the Mission – the two white wives and a Chinese servant called Song Lan, who was notoriously single. Dosed with opium, Mrs Gerrard felt no pain, although she was torn and therefore confined to bed. She was incensed, and the wives came to dread those lips grown thin on betrayal.

Near the end of her convalescence she took short walks with a guidebook but without her infant. She ignored the temple of Kam-fa which, said the book, was 'of no particular interest, further than its being the temple of the goddess of mothers and children'. Opposite, however, was a large granite well with a curious dragon design: 'This is worth seeing.' She returned with a box of dominoes and a back-scratcher at fifty cents each, a pillow made of porcelain at ten cents, and a fan, also ten cents.

Her purchases were suddenly more expensive. The ladies disputed whether they signified an interest in China or preparations for her departure, but agreed that they were unsuitable: an opium pipe for one dollar; an opium set for two smokers, complete, at ten dollars; an executioner's sword, one dollar. They no longer challenged her intention to go home, though their husbands repeated that China pined for the one God and that many missionaries had need of a life's companion.

The arguments half worked: Mrs Gerrard disappeared but left her baby, a note pinned to his smock revealing that she was leaving for an unspecified destination under the protection of a ship's officer, who had thus shown himself to be 'the truest kind of Christian gentleman'.

John's substitute mother was Song Lan. She had been part of the Mission for a year, at first sitting silently at the back of the hall during daily prayers. 'I have stopped believing in idols and spirits,' she said, and the Mission was charmed by her frankness.

She worked in the kitchens of a rich river trader but came each afternoon to stare at the Chinese Bible, printed in Japan between wooden covers and the size of a suitcase. She wished to be baptized, but was told that she must first learn the Gospel message: she could read only the common shop signs, however, and her studies lagged.

The women of the Mission took the Word to local

wives in their homes. Song Lan, becoming anxious, volunteered to help. But she hated the knots of characters in the Chinese Bible and forgot the Gospel story at once. 'I am forty years old and will soon die,' she said. 'Let me do something.'

She would wash and cook and sew, she decided – anything the Mission wished, and again without pay. Her offer was generous: the Chinese knew poverty too well to give away their labour. But still the Mission wavered.

Its president, Mr Burkett, tested her knowledge of the Gospel, but Song Lan began to cry. 'Will the Mission pray after my death,' she said, 'and make offerings for my spirit?'

Now Burkett understood. Song Lan had been sold as a child and had no relations. She had never married and was too poor to buy a son. With no one to light lamps and give offerings, she would be a beggar in the spirit kingdom, wandering in the cold and dark. At last, mad with grief and rage, she would return as a hungry ghost, doing harm in the kingdom of the living.

Song Lan knew how loneliness poisons the heart and had tried to stay good. How could she contemplate an afterlife of evil? And how consoling was Mr Burkett as he recited our Saviour's promise.

'In my Father's house are many mansions,' he said as Song Lan knelt and wept. 'I go to prepare a place for you. I will come again, and receive you unto myself.'

She became the Mission's amah, which John's childish tongue pronounced as 'mama'. The Mission had many young charges, though it preferred them older than John:

babies, after all, needed such a long investment. It scooped abandoned children from the streets or bought them from their indigent parents. It fed the waifs and strays, shamelessly buying souls with rice, preaching as they ate or as they dozed around the coal stove in winter, so that local people said the Christians used children's eyes to make silver for their mirrors. Why else would they want such creatures?

But the Mission was thinking of the future, when these infants would disarm China's great objection to the Gospel – that it was the creed of foreign demons. And it was remarkable how cheaply such children could be raised, provided one used native helpers like Song Lan.

In the Mission's register she was classified as Christian, but owed this distinction to the normal eclecticism of Chinese worship: she was soothed by a worn wooden Buddha, smooth as a thumb in her apron pocket; she whispered to a Cantonese spirit of the ashes when she cooked in the basement kitchen next to the nursery; she bowed secretly to a stone shelf over the oven, where the kitchen god had presided until expelled by the Jesus-worshippers; and she shuddered at the stories of Christ on the cross, wondering at a Lord of the Dead who let himself be tortured.

At last, learning that Jesus had walked on the lake at Galilee, she remembered him when she took letters on the swaying overloaded ferry to the Mission House in Hong Kong. Given the Mission's chronic lack of women, this was enough to qualify her as nursemaid for the child.

No one noticed a similar pantheism in young John.

He attended the Mission's austere worship, where there was no ceremony or singing, only declarations that the Bible was all. He learnt his Scriptures and listened respectfully when the white people told him about heaven and hell. And at night in the dormitory he stared at the Bible text on the wall above the oil lamp, which said, 'By the word of the Lord were the heavens made; and all the host of them by the breath of his mouth', which – said Mr Burkett – meant that God had created the world by speaking it, so that the world was a word.

Sometimes, though, this text was very fearsome, because it meant that everything was only a twist of air, and that John too was insubstantial and might be gathered back to heaven like the dew.

At such times the oil lamp only multiplied the shadows, which were busy with Chinese spirits that rustled with the roaches in the dry toilet, were couched in glory on the charcoal in the kitchen, and coiled in a whispering nest under his cot, their murmurs growing sinister until Song Lan gave him sugar cane smeared with opium paste, after which their muttering was louder but couldn't touch him.

He was her safeguard. She disliked the other children, the scrapings of the streets, but the white boy would surely tend her spirit.

She listened politely to Mr Burkett's stories about the spirit world where Jesus awaited her, welcoming all who were Christian, but in the evening she turned to John, who – like the all-knowing Lao Tze – had been born with the white hair of wisdom. 'Never forget me,' she said.

'Remember to pray for me, and light incense, and save my soul from wandering.'

She spoke in Cantonese, which was John's mother tongue: he knew English but it didn't fit his gestures. And he disliked books: he learnt English and Chinese scripts, but the shapes were a fence that he peered through. He was the only white child in class, smirking with his friends when Mr Burkett taught them in a mincing Cantonese, his dentures whistling.

One day he wept because of his pale hair, and Song took him across the river to a modest gate, then through shading banyans and tiny courtyards to the Ocean Banner Monastery and the statues of the Kings of Heaven. One had a green face and controlled the winds; one with a red face controlled the elements of air, fire and water; the dark-faced one, holding a pearl in one hand and a golden dragon in the other, ruled the weather. But it was to the fourth that she dedicated the youngster, because this god – the lord of rain and rivers – also had a white face: John touched his forehead to the ground, next to the point of the god's handsome umbrella, but wept on the ferry home because his hair wasn't cured.

He began creeping out with his friends, a blanket over his Western clothes, a cap over his hair, his blonde brows like the shaved brows of the natives. They slipped from the dormitory window, barefoot, dropping from an outhouse roof to a teeming alley, then taking a regular route through the street of the porcelain makers, past the traders in human hair, peering into the shop of Koo Mow, which was hung with birds' nests from the caves of Borneo, and visiting the pigs which crouched in baskets outside the slaughterhouse, their eyes sewn shut.

A bridge marked the border of the European quarter. Here a watchman fired his cannon at 9 p.m., and they competed to be furthest from the dull report, swimming in some foul canal or treading an alley in the Chinese city, hurrying home as incense sticks were lit by every door, skipping under shoulder poles, leaping the baskets of the street vendors, pausing at the more fearsome shrines where John nodded and his friends bowed. He pulled their pigtails and they snatched his cap.

Their favourite temple had paintings of the chambers of the Buddhist hell. In one, animals took revenge on meat-eaters, so that chickens boiled human limbs, cows on their hind legs struck off heads, and men were hung by the heels and disembowelled by top-hatted pigs: the vegetarian elect were carried to heaven by the creatures they had spared. They sniggered at the newer chambers of hell where those who adopted Western ways must dance for ever on red-hot boards while cigarettes burned their mouths and female devils proffered drinks of molten copper.

The boys outgrew this tameness, squeezing into the courtroom where prisoners knelt on chains and broken glass, or were hung up by a hand, or had their mouths whipped and their ankles smashed. They followed their favourites to the prison, mingling with visitors and pointing through the wooden bars, and thence to the potters' field, where they crawled to the front of the crowd to stand on hot jars, fresh from the ovens, and watched their heroes kneel for the headsman. A parricide was tied on a cross for the death of a thousand cuts, and the boys talked about Jesus.

In the classroom John was still mocked for his strange hair and he still dipped pigtails into ink, stuck pencils in pigtails, trapped pigtails in desks, or tied boys together by their pigtails. Then some of his classmates changed to short hair and Western clothes and grew solemn, having given themselves to Christ.

But his best friends vanished for ever into the streets, pigtails flying, where now he couldn't go. He still wore a cap, but was too tall to merge into crowds and was followed by mutterings of 'Foreign demon' and 'Kill!' and was once chased by beaten stragglers from the Boxer Rising. Children were shielded from his glittering eyes, cats were afraid and dogs barked. In public toilets where he had flicked the little white maggots at his friends, no one sat next to him.

He was obliged to read. The Mission library was only a shelf in a corridor, since anything but the Bible might mislead, but there was a startling volume, nibbled by beetles, about missionaries who stained themselves with tea to map forbidden provinces – counting their paces with a rosary, measuring altitude with the boiling point of their kettle, their compass in a false-bottomed bag – until they were heroically lost and bamboo grew through their bones.

Often they were murdered. He crouched by a window in the corridor, frowning with effort, moving his finger along the lines of a report by the Catholic Church into the death in Kwangsi province in 1857 of Abbé Chapdeleine, whose heart was torn out of his chest 'and, still beating, chopped into pieces, fried in a pan with pig's grease, and eaten'. A fresh newspaper cutting told how the Boxers killed forty-five Christians in the courtyard of the governor's building in Taiyuan, a witness reporting, 'Mrs Farthing held the hands of her children, but the soldiers parted them and with one blow beheaded her. The executioner beheaded all the children and did it skilfully, but the soldiers were clumsy. Mrs Lovitt said, "We came to China to bring you the good news of Jesus Christ. We have done you no harm, only good, why do you treat us so?" A soldier took off her spectacles before beheading her. All were surprised at the firmness and quietness of the foreigners, none of whom except two or three of the children made any noise.'

He began to teach, at first confined to the infants' class, then promoted to the seniors, where the girls asked him many questions about Adam and Eve and could laugh without breathing. He burned with desire and knew himself desired, but could see no chance of satisfaction.

He worked all day at his teaching or secretarial tasks, but went out after dark and thought himself dangerous. He stared over the foul river, thinking how Westerners sneered at the missionaries and the Chinese hated them, except for the converts, who were in some way stupid. He thought of the richer Mission Houses, which were received at consulates and sent missionaries upriver and had rich friends in the West who left bequests.

He went back to the Ocean Banner Monastery but bowed only from politeness at the white-faced statue, passing instead to a five-sided pagoda where the Lord Buddha was carved: a bowl of water stood by his marble toes to show the purity of his thought, though it squirmed with mosquito larvae.

He walked the mud flats where corpses congregated from upstream, dumped into the river by landless peasants or the victims of bandits and obscenely mutilated. Once a Chinese gunboat exploded, and dead soldiers gathered against the mud like new land. The boat had blown up at night when the soldiers had loosened their belts, though their ankle straps were still tied: now their trousers floated behind them and their pigtails were unbraided as if the river had undressed them. Sometimes there were drowned women. He bought a pipe and spat with Chinese skill.

All this was the sign of a healthy spirit, said Burkett, who thought himself a manly man. He clapped John's broad back and called him 'our Adonis', then smiled and turned away as John looked down at his baldness.

But one day Burkett led him to a gloomy sitting room. Outside the door he gave a short laugh and said, 'You must not think of this as any kind of arrangement, as with our Chinese brothers. The choice is yours, of course.'

He opened the door to disclose a Chinese girl with a round face. She was sitting by the window and stared outside as Burkett made the introductions. Her name, it emerged, was Grace.

At last she turned to John. She looked up his long body and ran out of breath before she reached the top. Burkett saw that his plan would work, but was nonetheless irritated.

Her eyes were small for a Westerner, big for an Oriental, but her hair was thoroughly Chinese. She had styled it for this meeting, but it had frizzed like champagne. Burkett, startled, had likened her to 'one of our African sisters'. Grace had tried to flatten the frizz with water, the only cosmetic allowed, but couldn't be sure of her success: there were no mirrors in Mission buildings.

'You have met before,' said Burkett, and Grace scowled with shyness. They had spent an hour together as children, it seemed, and John remembered a girl who had cried as he played. Suddenly, with a snort of laughter, Burkett left them. They drank tea for an agonizing few minutes. She was reassured. He seemed clumsy but well-meaning. He was so beautiful.

John was breathless with desire. He had walked by the prostitutes in the alleys off the river frontage, and stared at the flower girls in their covered skiffs, their faces glowing as they sang under coloured lanterns. One night he had stepped on to the water, striding from hull to hull across a suburb of boats as the prostitutes squealed and their keepers cursed, reaching a ruined fishing boat where an old man gave him wine, then woke him by fumbling in his trousers, for what purpose John didn't wait to discover.

The prospect of a wife, and all that followed, was astonishing to him. He grew dizzy that this girl had been brought to him, sat in a building he knew, might share his bed. And marriage would save him from appetites which surely were abnormally intense. The only Western women he knew were Mission wives, brisk and undesirable, but Grace was half Chinese: he remembered a woman in a doorway, stupid with opium, grubby fingers proffering her flesh.

Grace stayed in Canton for a week, and they walked along the riverfront without a chaperone because the Mission believed in the nobility of the individual. She was surprised that John had received so little instruction in his teaching duties, and at last he replied, 'Perhaps I need a helpmate.' In this way their marriage was settled.

Burkett explained their mission. They would go upriver to a fishing settlement which should be a suitable base for evangelism. If necessary they could then explore further.

John looked forward to this adventure. As to its purpose – the spreading of God's word – his feelings were complicated but included surges of devotion, as a man brings gifts to the lover he betrays.

It was the first inland mission for a decade from the Canton Mission House, and John's training was again inadequate, comprising a meeting with Burkett – at which he was warned about the importance of accounts and the temptations of Eastern women – and a week at an outstation on the plains near Canton, whose principal had a worrying reputation as a sportsman. Sure enough, John went out with the principal at dawn each day, returning at dusk with his pockets full of snipe, his ankles scratched raw on rice stubble, and his great limbs for the first time weary.

He came back to Canton in the principal's old fishing hat, given as a souvenir for 'a most promising young outdoorsman' and unused on the region's filthy ditches so that a rusty hook lay forgotten in its brim and its tweed still smelled of Connecticut trout, which was Song Lan's excuse when she burned it in her jealousy.

She would not see Grace, who was stealing him for the creed which forgot its dead, and did not attend their wedding, though it was held in the Mission House and was notably short and austere.

Then she fell ill, and John asked to postpone his mission. Regrettably, said Mr Burkett, too many arrangements had been made. But her sickness was terrible, the spirit coughed drop by drop from the flesh. In her weeks of drowning Song Lan extracted more promises from John, which he couldn't reconcile with the teachings of Jesus. He held the basin for her blood and called her 'amah', using his old pronunciation.

'Fear not, my young John,' said Burkett. 'Your beloved amah will be tended by my own wife.'

Like her husband, Mrs Burkett had been broken by the beastliness of China. It would be bearable if the place were merely poor: but the triumph of dirt and ignorance, as if celebrated, that was the hard thing. She would do her best for Song Lan but the end couldn't be far off, with all the exhausting funeral arrangements. It was exasperating that John and his wife were leaving. 'An outcast and a half-caste,' she said, and her husband did not rebuke her.

'It is a thrilling venture,' Burkett told John, 'for which your health, strength, and knowledge of native customs and language – which you share with your new wife – so amply equip you.' But another way to see it was that Burkett's meagre bribes had secured a site amongst the unregarded river folk.

2

Like a man surveying his fields, John looked over the pebble beach, the broad river and the three boats of the fisher folk. He was handsome and strong, not made for this backwater. But he was young: first came an apprenticeship.

'It's very small,' said Grace. 'Astonishingly small.' She had expected a minor town, with many souls to win for the Lord. Instead, from the veranda of their new house, she looked down at half a dozen huts on stilts.

She glanced at her husband, thinking that this was their first proper home: an ordinary bride would wish to be carried across the threshold. But the custom was very likely pagan. It was best to be safe.

She went inside. Directly through the front door was a sitting room with a window to the veranda and a view of the river. It held a low table, two upright chairs and a chest of drawers. Beyond was a kitchen with a table and three wobbly stools. Grace pushed through a ragged curtain and found the narrow bedroom down the side of the house.

'Where is Yue Fat?' she demanded.

'Ah, fat Yue Fat,' said John. They had decided that an Imperial tax collector would be carried everywhere, eating Turkish delight and fanned with ostrich feathers.

'They have stolen the pork,' Grace said angrily,

staring round the kitchen. 'Those wretched muleteers.' She lifted a sack: beneath were the square tins of pork.

John had gone out through the kitchen door. He crouched down, looking under the house: it rested on wooden piles driven into the slope, but there was nowhere to hide their money. He went back to the kitchen: perhaps they could put the cash behind a brick in the oven.

'Oh, honourable missie,' he called, wheedling.

'Yes?' said Grace from the bedroom.

'Honolabur missie. Prease, pletty missie.'

'What!'

'I want to shave my face so prease make water in a bowl for me.' She was silent but, he hoped, amused. She was unpredictable on such matters.

They spent an hour unpacking, then saw that the fishing boats had landed. John said, 'They are curious about us, I think.'

'Perhaps we should go down,' said Grace, but at once became shy. She must tidy the house, she declared.

John paused on the veranda, admiring the river, a hundred yards wide and brown as a ploughed field. He hoped for much sport. He went down the steep path which, he saw, became a stream in the wet season. At the edge of the beach was a bush. In its branches were dried-out twigs and scraps of grass, no doubt left in early summer, when the river was swollen by meltwater from the mountains. He was reassured. The river was too wide here for serious floods.

Grace, exasperated at her shyness, fussed in the house or peered from the veranda at the fisher folk drawing their boats up the beach. The women would be her responsibility: John would hire a boat to go fishing, thereby gaining an entrée with the men.

Only one man was visible on the beach. She watched John approach him and talk. They climbed a ladder into one of the huts.

She waited for her husband to emerge, then checked the provisions from Canton which the muleteers had carried unwillingly to the kitchen: bottles of iodine and bicarbonate, dried fruit, tins of beans and stewed lamb, the vexatious pork. And they had acquired supplies during their journey: dried ducks and fish, a side of bacon, two pheasants which she hung over the door, sacks of rice, and cabbages stacked like cannonballs. She found rat holes in the walls, which would have to be blocked. She had nails and tin for the purpose.

She looked again for her husband, then dragged the mattress from the bed, ready to be burnt. Again she checked the beach, then rubbed Keating's Insect Powder into cracks in the bed frame and set four tin dishes under its legs. She would fill them with lamp oil, so that nothing could crawl from the floor.

Suddenly, with a hiss of impatience, she left the house. She glanced at the colossal scree slopes on the far bank, then at the line of stilted huts along the beach, then looked again for her husband. She set off down the slope, her knees trembling because she was nervous and the slope was steep. She pretended she was going for water:

she had their new steel bucket, which she carried in her hand because a shoulder pole was too Chinese.

A couple of fisher women sat by a fire on the beach. Annoyed by their frank gaze, she hesitated. Again she looked for her husband, then went to the upstream limit of the huts. The bucket clanked and she thought of her refusal to bring a native helper. In Canton the idea had seemed heroic, but perhaps the locals would merely think her insignificant.

A faint path from the beach climbed a headland no taller than herself. The path made a shortcut to the upstream end of the beach, where she found two more women, one drawing water, the other, a little way down-stream, rinsing clothes. As Grace filled her bucket she heard them speaking a kind of Cantonese, though with a heavy accent.

The women saw her. There was some muttering, and they walked past with faces turned away. She should have talked to them about the Gospel, she thought, and perhaps given them leaflets. She went back to the beach, where the four women watched her from the fire. Where was her husband? Blushing, she climbed to the house.

She stood in the living room, then went to the veranda, watching for John. She went back to the living room and stood with her hands gripped together. She said aloud, 'I am very foolish.' She went out on to the veranda, hesitated, then hurried back down the slope, this time carrying the leaflets.

For some reason she had brought the full bucket. From their places around the fire the four women watched her approach. She put down the bucket, which tipped on the pebbles, splashing the leaflets. She nodded at the women and tried to smile.

'I come with news of the one God, who loves everyone,' she said. She began handing out the leaflets, which showed an image of Christ with his hand lifted in blessing: below were the words 'God loves us all', though no doubt the women couldn't read.

They watched silently, their hands around wooden cups, but took the leaflets with polite nods. One said, 'How her hands are soft! Surely her husband is rich, with many servants.'

'Not rich, not rich,' said Grace.

There was another silence until they again took pity on her: one said, 'In your country, do the women not wear trousers?'

Grace explained that this was almost unknown, and women wore a dress or skirt like some women in the hill tribes. She foresaw the next question.

'Surely this is immodest. Do their husbands not complain?'

'Husbands complain about everything,' said Grace, and provoked laughter. She was reminded of John: at last he was coming across the beach.

'He is the headman,' said John. 'He has agreed. I'll go fishing with him.'

'You were some time,' said Grace, sounding irritable because she was nervous.

But John was staring at the slope above their house.

Against the sky, a blob of vivid red appeared. Squinting against the light, they saw a man in a silk tunic. Behind him came a pair of soldiers, then an insignificant figure in black or grey.

They were pleased to see that the man in red was fat.

The collector had brought tea. Grace and John, breathless from their dash up the slope, bowed the party into their house. Yue Fat and his secretary sat primly while the two soldiers – a young private and a shrivelled old sergeant – laid out food from a covered tray.

Yue Fat tried not to stare: he had seen white people in Canton, but never so close. The male barbarian lifted his feet like a prancing Manchu pony, with none of the smooth gliding of a mandarin. The woman's eyes were wet and bulging like a tongue. In confusion he dropped his gaze, and was confronted by her long feet, bony as the river fish.

Fortunately he could keep his head bowed, because his secretary was bringing the couple's things. First the little man showed him John's comb and razor, which had lain beside the wash bowl, spreading them on his master's lap. Next he found the Sheffield knives and forks which Grace had bought as a treat at a ship's chandlers in Hong Kong. 'Like butcher's tools,' thought Yue Fat: and how did the foreigners not stab their lips?

'My master likes these items very much,' said the little secretary brightly.

Grace said, 'Thank you,' and fell determinedly silent.

The secretary bent his head to his master's murmurings: he turned to the Westerners and said, 'My master would like the comb.'

'I'm afraid that's impossible,' said Grace.

The secretary was nonplussed. 'My master has thought carefully. You can use the brush.'

Grace said nothing.

'You see I knew many missionaries in Hong Kong,' said the secretary, irritated. 'They were always most polite.' It took Grace and John a moment to notice a remarkable change.

'You speak English,' said Grace with astonishment. 'Are you a Christian?'

'Perhaps and perhaps not,' said the little man.

'So, excuse me, why did you come here?'

'I came because tax collectors are very important and must have a secretary.'

'But how well you speak our language!'

'Oh, how, how. So many questions!' He recovered and reverted to Cantonese. 'Please tell me if you enjoy your tea. And see the sweetmeats.' Indeed the Chinese had prepared a beautiful tea, with a charcoal burner and little cups and covered lacquered dishes holding sweets.

'And the people here, do they all speak Cantonese?' said Grace.

'Oh, very few,' said the secretary.

'And in the next valley?' said Grace. 'In the opium plantation?'

'Mostly tribes, in fact, with their own tongue. And

rather hazardous for outsiders. They are vulgar people, suspicious of those they do not know.'

'We will go there,' said Grace. 'And the fishing village here: is it really so small? That is, are there other inhabitants we have yet to see?'

The secretary laughed elegantly, but it seemed there would be no reply.

John was looking at Yue Fat, who ate and said nothing. He was scarcely older than themselves, and not really so fat. He had a little paunch and his face was very wide at the cheekbones, like a face in the back of a spoon, but he was tall with long round limbs. Still, he looked disagreeable, like a child who has overeaten and should be put to bed.

The secretary noticed his gaze. 'You are thinking about his name,' he said in English. 'Perhaps he should not learn your language.'

3

John and the headman grew used to fishing together. There was no friendliness, because the headman was too morose and too disturbed by the white man's eyes, pale as the eyes of a cat. His name was Sho.

Each morning John arrived with a hearty handshake, his scuffed boots planted like stones, his unvarying old jacket bulging with rice for them both, bottle corks stuck with hooks he had brought from Canton, and half a dozen raisins for little Shen, the headman's daughter. She couldn't yet speak, but laughed when she saw the white man and was always alert for his arrival, hidden behind the headman's wife but watching the Mission House for the great hunched figure to bustle out.

First John dragged the boat from its berth under the headman's house and down two slimy poles to the water's edge. Headman Sho, careful as an invalid, crept to his place amidships as John launched the boat into the sheltered water off the beach.

John leapt into the stern and the headman stood at the upright oars, scowling and tense, forcing the boat into the increasing current until they moved almost sideways, edging towards the far bank where the current was most vicious and made a kind of river within the river, its surface spiked.

Here Sho brought them to a huge boulder in the water. It had slid from the scree slope in his grandfather's time and had settled lower as the river burrowed under it, so that now it was low and smooth like a turtle's back. It had a submerged crevice where an intrepid forefather had jammed a pole. Sho slipped their prow rope over the pole, then they were swept downstream until the rope snapped tight, firing a line of droplets over the river.

They relaxed, though their boat bounced in the rough water behind the rock as if dragged by a ship, its flat bottom smacking the river, wings of water flapping out so that the four fisher women laughed. Their own boats were slim as fishes, and worked in the slower waters near the beach, tethered to wooden floats which led to anchor-stones on the riverbed.

Through the day the fisher folk let out their tethering ropes and used an oar to deflect their boats across the current, in this way patrolling the river and catching eel, bream, mandarin fish, and delicious catfish, John's favourite, which the fisher women sewed shut around sweet herbs and roasted over the driftwood fire.

The women caught a carp, trapping it between their two boats, beating the water to drive it to the shallows. It was fat as a monk, but headman Sho would not touch it: the fish had come from a paddy field downstream, he said, where cultivated fish swam among the rice, eating the farmers' excrement and full of worms which cooking didn't kill. He called the four women 'the old aunts' and shook his head in disgust.

But it was a fine thing to be on the water in the

strengthening sun, a cool wind flowing down the valley, and fish proffered on the open hand of the Father. John stood in the stern, knees flexed against the jarring of the boat as it belly-flopped into the waves, his line trailing behind with the hooks from Canton and the flashing lure he had made from a spoon, which he stabbed into the sand each morning to make it shine. The headman sat amidships, knees together like an invalid, glad of the white man's help but keeping his bare feet clear of John's boots.

'My God was a fisherman for a time,' said John, panting because the river was rough. 'He walked on the water, and helped His friends to catch mighty catches of fish.'

'He is like my god,' said headman Sho.

'That's true,' said John. 'But my God isn't just the god of fishing. He is the god of everything.'

Sho preferred a god's full attention, but only said, 'When your god walked on the water, was he barefoot?'

John laughed. But then he said, 'Yes, perhaps,' because he thought of Jesus walking like a masseur on the bare back of the water.

Next day he decided that headman Sho had been warning him about his boots, because one of the aunts gave him sandals. They had to be specially made at Market Village, she said: she had discovered his ridiculous size by measuring his boot-prints in the sand.

'Wonderful,' said John. 'Now I won't be drowned by these horrible black anchors.' The sandals were beaten bamboo, as soft as cloth. They gripped on the slimy planks of the boat and he wore them with delight, his linen trousers turned up, his jacket off and his shirtsleeves rolled. The sandals were like the cool mountain wind.

Each day before their fishing, John climbed the ladder of the headman's house. He told Grace it was for a bowl of warm water and a discussion of fishing matters. She said, 'You also discuss the Gospel, of course,' and John nodded and said, 'Certainly.'

Headman Sho had indeed become religious. Noting his failing strength, he was scrupulous about the ceremony before each day's fishing. This had once been a mere bow to the household shrine and a salutation to the forefathers: now, with an old man's insomnia, he rose early and spent hours at his devotions, though his young wife grumbled from the bed and little Shen sneezed in the incense smoke.

He told the fish god about the previous day's catch, down to the last fingerling, and if the fish was big he laid it all night in front of the shrine so that the god could mourn. 'I am a poor man,' said Sho. 'I and my wife and child must eat, therefore we have taken your soldier with many regrets.'

He brought John into the house to show that the giant meant no insult to the god, although his wife said that the barbarian's eyelashes were white as a pig's, that their house would break under his weight, and that his white-yellow hair was a sign of disease, the man having been exiled here like a leper.

So John stood each day before the little shrine, though

he refused the ribbons which the headman proffered. He smiled to show his distance from the rites, staring instead around the tiny hut, which was neat and pleasing, the shape of a tent, its walls and roof of yellow thatch bound with reeds, its bamboo floor creaking like a basket, the fire in its box of earth, and the roof so low that the headman could only stand in the centre of its single room. He looked too at the headman's pretty wife, her head bowed, her grubby schoolgirl fingers insinuating as water among the threads of her mending.

Then the headman knelt and whispered, so that John felt the stirring of China's gods, who had crouched in the dark since before Jesus. He remembered his amah, who would soon be in their power and had begged for his help. He closed the mat door, bizarrely light: it would be terrible if Grace should see him.

4

Grace's grandfather had been a prey to enthusiasms. He was a London merchant, a widower, and became inspired by the link between free trade and social progress. He held soirées at his Belgravia mansion, where indignant refugees spoke of their homelands and grew impassioned as the wine went round.

He had long been involved in the China trade, but only now noted the struggle of its people to throw off the dead hand of feudalism. He knew several traders in Hong Kong and one sent his second son to study in London. How charming were the boy's mistakes with the language, how straight his back in a fine London suit, and how black his eyes as he watched the merchant's daughter over the rim of his glass.

Their engagement was a great shock. The merchant tried to reconcile himself, visiting his many friends to reveal this ultimate proof of free-thinking, once bringing his latest curio, a straw hat bought from a Chinese sailor in the Charing Cross Road.

'It's the only sensible hat ever made,' he declared, showing how the brim was short at the front and back but swept out in wings at the side, thus protecting the shoulders. But his friends saw his empty eyes and said nothing.

At Southampton he watched his only child wave from the ship's rail, and couldn't wave back. On the journey home he thought of his empty house and the gifts from his son-in-law's family ranged in the second lounge. He saw how he might comfort himself with their startling luxury, then grew afraid.

His daughter's first letters spoke of the warmth of her husband's family and her pleasure in the new culture she must acquire. But then she wrote another letter, requesting funds to buy a passage to England. Her new home allowed no secrets: the letter was discovered and her husband insisted – without passion – that she wrote a more acceptable version.

Her father read this letter but didn't keep it, finding its conventional phrases a further rebuff. He had thought often of her delight as she waved from the ship at Southampton: the joy of any bride, he saw, was an insult to her parents, the more so when it involved such a separation. In his answering letter he spoke of a woman, remarkable for her good sense, who had become 'more than a friend'.

For his daughter, these two letters were the death of hope. Her husband was the first foreigner she had met after her awakening, and she fell in love because his English was bad: their words were as simple as the words of children or saints, soul speaking to soul. In Hong Kong they had married again, this time in the Chinese style amid bewildering pomp. No questions were asked of bride and groom during the ceremony, which seemed a touching presumption of the truth in their hearts. Later she recalled that Chinese marriages are settled by the parents.

She turned her attention to the marital home, the arena of every bride's ambitions. At first she was not afraid. Her father was rich and she would buy cutlery to end the agony of chopsticks, a Western bathroom instead of the humiliations of the Chinese toilette, and a little carriage for journeys with the white acquaintances she would shortly make.

But her home was one in a maze of tiny apartments. Uncounted siblings and cousins had other rooms round other yards, and the boundaries of their suites were unclear and caused her many embarrassments. She retreated to her own apartment, its wooden rooms creaking like cabins as she squirmed on black-wood benches made of right-angles.

Her excursions brought no relief. In a closed sedan, her maids walking behind to answer every need, she shrank from the headlong streets and thought again of the intractable house. What could she do, since her husband administered her money and her plans would anyway be blocked by her mother-in-law?

This lady had been as shocked by the marriage as the English merchant, with less reason to expect or indulge it. In her husband's rare visits from his life of business and concubines they spoke much about the misalliance, and she had to shelter their son from his father's wrath: she thus became reconciled, and received the tall pale stranger with sympathy. She was startled by the white girl's hunger for change, but – calm in her power – smiled fondly at this passionate new creature, and denied her everything.

Her son had laid aside his radicalism and his Western clothes, and was bored by his wife's misery. He withdrew to a conventional distance, leaving her to fret alone. He attended only to the wishes of his mother, whose requirements were infrequent but absolute. He was, after all, only the second son.

The white woman fell pregnant. She noted the new interest of her maids and mother-in-law, and hated her own gratitude. Disappointment naturally followed the birth of a girl. No one felt this more than the young mother, who showed what she had learnt of China: she ate two balls of opium with a glass of wine and died without pain.

The infant seemed destined for obscurity, since her father was seeking another bride. Meanwhile the wet nurse complained of her gross appetite and strange odour, and yearned for news from the barbarian grandfather.

A letter came: the old man spoke of his grief but added that after twenty years as a widower he was marrying again. The arrangements were consuming a great deal of time.

With enormous effort, a young nurse was hired from the American missionary school. She had no knowledge of Oriental babies, and noted how white was the infant's skin: surely she would not prosper in a Chinese home.

She too wrote to the English grandfather, who – like his son-in-law – was cured of radicalism. A photograph of his daughter had stood by his bed, but was now exiled to a cold sitting room. Even so, he was consumed by pulses of anger: she had been killed by barbaric ignorance and pride. His reply to the missionary was brief but accompanied by a rather longer letter from his solicitor, setting out an offer.

Grace was moved to the Mission House. Her Chinese grandmother regretted that the child would take no part in honouring the ancestors, including eventually her own spirit, but she had grown away from the infant in the months while they awaited news from England. In any case, there were four fat grandsons to lead such ceremonies.

Grace's new home was a bustling place in a Chinese sector. Great banners adorned its frontage, calling the world to Jesus, and inside were two schoolrooms, a Dispensary-Hospital with six beds, and a dormitory where a cot was installed and she was fussed over by the wives and patted by absent-minded men.

Her pale skin was not rare among Eastern babies and darkened swiftly. But the besotted women nevertheless dressed her in a starched and frilly skirt and tied her bobbed hair with a pink ribbon: there was, after all, the matter of her grandfather's quarterly contribution, which had already allowed the dispatch upstream of three missionaries and their native helpers.

By the age of seven she was speaking of 'the Chinese' with the bland aloofness which white children acquire despite the most enlightened teachers. But she had a fright when taken to see her grandmother, an incomprehensible Oriental, shrivelled as a nut, dying on enormous cushions in a maze of wooden rooms.

She dreamt of these rooms and of a struggle to escape, waking in fear and calming herself with the text on the dormitory wall, which said: 'The Word became flesh and dwelt amongst us.' This meant Jesus, she knew: God had spoken a word which became our Saviour walking in the world. She pictured Jesus all golden and striding like a capital letter in an old Bible: one day she would marry such a man.

So Grace survived her fears and sat once more at the dinner table in the evening, the starched linen in her lap, swinging her feet in their shiny Western boots, then kneeling in the dormitory in her crisp white nightdress, knowing she was longer at her prayers than the other girls, not least because of the exhaustive list of names on whom she called God's blessing, including the Chinese servants who sighed and muttered as they waited to turn down the lamp. She rode in sedan chairs with the white women, feeling herself a kind of mascot, but was not seen outdoors with the men since this had led to ugly interventions from passers-by.

Other problems began. She would creep into the servants' quarters to consult a mirror. How Chinese she was! Her teachers rebuked her for feeling her scalp: she was searching for the first fine wisps which would mean that her hair was turning European.

She avoided the Chinese when possible, and grew disappointed with the women of the Mission, who said they were in loco parentis, which seemed to mean only that they attracted all her resentment. She sought friendships among the city's secular Westerners, but

42

was rebuffed: missionaries were lower-class cranks who enraged the natives. So she took tea at the household of the missionary Bishop of Victoria and made the acquaintance of the two ladies of the Baxter Girls' School Trust. She wrote cards to introduce herself to the London Missionary Society, the Irish Presbyterian Mission, the Joyful News Mission, the American Methodist Girls' School, the Church Missionary Society, and the Wesleyan, Basel and Baptist missions. But the cards were found in the post room and confiscated, being a kind of disloyalty.

Still, the Mission enjoyed an intermittent supply of young women from Europe and America, and Grace gave them definitive statements on local customs, diet and religion, which she called superstition. She affected an amusement, which rose to hilarity on such matters as foot-binding and the eating of dogs. But the women grew quiet when she laughed, so instead she was cool and disapproving.

One young woman spoke in tongues, rolling her eyes up while friends restrained her amazing strength: by contrast she was a little superior as she explained that such displays were now common in the chapel attached to the Mission's New York headquarters. The women of the Mission House thought they heard Cantonese in her inspired speech, and remembered the old idea that this was the tongue spoken by Adam and Eve. But then it was learnt that the woman had taken Cantonese lessons in America, and only Grace retained an interest in the links between China and the Bible lands, and was even a little reconciled to her own mixed blood.

The young women went upriver, where her knowledge proved unreliable. They returned to Hong Kong only to convalesce or on their passage home, and preferred not to talk of their adventures. During the Boxer Rising they came with their families and slept in the schoolroom, the women weeping and whispering, though not to her, while their horrid offspring ran wild. Three boys, tanned and no doubt verminous, said that the heads of native converts had been nailed by the ears to railings around their school: they played baseball in a corridor with the great black Bible for a base, and Grace was obliged to tell the principal.

Outside was the pagan vigour of Hong Kong, whose new wealth eclipsed Canton. The Mission relaxed in this bustle, perhaps feeling itself less observed, and its library showed this ease: she read Shakespeare and Austen, whose heroines were loved for their wit, and briefly adopted the library, laying its books in the sun to discourage mould, watching the wind fumble through the pages, and varnishing the covers against roaches, which had an odd preference for green and brown.

There was a little tendon at the corner of her eyes, which she would twist and stretch as she read and reread the Bible which bore her mother's name. She thought she smelled a Western scent, and wondered at the tiny grubbiness at the edge of its pages. She lay in bed reading, stretching her eyelids till sleep possessed her.

The Mission baptized by adult immersion. In Canton, John was brought to the river by Mr Burkett, whose distaste for China had produced a neat technique: his palm covered the mouth while his thumb and forefinger pinched shut the nostrils. In Hong Kong, Grace waited on the muddy bank and recalled the charcoal filters and boiling pans which purified their water, the alum which cleared its sediment, the bleach which killed its germs, and how their only palatable water was the rain captured in great pots which were sealed with parchment to keep out mosquitoes. But her young baptizer thought only of God, tipping her backwards in the shallows till China's foul effluvia shut like a book above her.

Then her grandfather died. There was talk of a will, and for a few weeks she felt suspended. She was called to the principal's office and discovered that she owned a large house by the Thames, with a cash sum to sustain her in England until she found employment.

'My home is China,' she said, having rehearsed her answer. 'I bestow this bequest on the Mission House, so that it may help the great work of bringing the Word of God to our Chinese brethren.' The principal only nodded, and she was disappointed.

John was like a thunderbolt. On the night of their betrothal she lay in bed reading the Song of Solomon: 'Thou art beautiful, O my love, terrible as an army with banners. A bundle of myrrh is my well-beloved unto me; he shall lie all night betwixt my breasts.'

She whispered as if to a lover, and heard how the word 'whispered' was like the word 'breasts'.

5

Every morning Grace cooked rice, which John carried in their shiny bucket to the fisher folk, who were too busy to talk. While they fished, she fussed around the house, worried that there was so little to do, watching her husband on the dreadful river, and the headman's strange wife wandering the beach.

Later she cooked more rice for the fisher folk, who came ashore in midafternoon and spent the rest of the day cleaning their catch and mending equipment. The headman ignored her, scooping rice with his face turned away, then working on his boat with John. But the four aunts sat around the fire on rocks padded with grass discs, and were happy to talk.

She was asked why her father liked fishing. Grace said that John was her husband not her father: he was not old, despite his white hair.

'And this village?' she said, seizing her chance. 'I have seen only one father here and one child. Perhaps the other men have gone to fish elsewhere, or are trading or hunting or visiting relatives?'

'All dead,' said the aunts, eyes downcast.

One day, they said, a husband had watery bowels and soon all the men and children were dead. The tax collector left in a panic with his soldiers – 'not this tax collector, the thief, but the one before' – so that they had lived in terror of bandits, and two of the women had been sick and sat outside their houses in the weak spring sun, waiting to recover or to follow their families into the river.

'Men die,' said an aunt.

'Yes,' said another. 'They boast and fight, but then they die and the river takes them away.'

'Well,' said Grace, 'you know that only their bodies go down the river. Their souls go to our Lord Jesus in heaven, and will wait for you there.'

'Certainly. And meanwhile we hope for handsome young men to come along the river.'

'But we are too old now, so they don't want us.'

'We have the boats, though, and our houses.'

'Yes, so we are waiting for handsome young men who are poor.'

'And young men always like fish,' said an aunt, as if this was a great joke.

'God's son had many friends who were fisher folk,' said Grace, 'He asked them to spread His message. He said, "I will make you fishers of men."'

'Our husbands never allowed us in the boats, because there is bad luck between a woman and boats. But then they died and we had no choice.'

'We had no choice. Our husbands were dead.'

'At first we wanted to cast a line from the beach, but we had no bait. So we walked into the shallows with the net, but our arms were too short or too weak or too crooked.'

'The net only caught ourselves.'

'Yes, yes,' said an aunt, leaping up to seize a net with the hands of an adept. She spun it above her head and let its weighted hem spin down and around her like a dancer's dress, so that she was wrapped in its white folds.

'Look, a silkworm!' said the others.

'Then these two useless ones tried to use a boat.'

'We were useless! We stayed near the beach, but still we couldn't steer.'

'We splashed with the oar, but the boat went round and round.'

'We cried and splashed because we were old and stupid and had no husbands.'

'And the boat leaked.'

'The planks had dried and shrunk, but we were too stupid to understand. We thought the river god was offended.'

'But it didn't matter because there were lots of fish.'

'Yes, the fish had bred while we were crying. And we were lucky and threw the net over a shoal of little fish.'

'So we could eat at last.' The four women were silent, thinking of these first fingerlings, which they had eaten raw, heads and all, gathering driftwood with trembling hands to grill even more, though they were so full they could hardly walk.

'And one of the big fish came into the shallows. A stupid big fish!'

'Sticking its nose in the shallows! Poking where it shouldn't!'

'We stabbed it with the spear. It was careless because no one had been fishing.'

'It swam under the boat and we stabbed it. It tore away, but it was too hurt.'

'Next day we saw it under the boat again. A big lump was loose off its side, with all the little fish nibbling. It couldn't move, so we threw the net over it.'

'It was surprised.' They laughed, remembering that first big fish as they dragged it ashore, how it had goggled at this conclave of women, so that they laughed and were drenched as they pushed their hands in its gills.

'What a miracle, too!' said one. 'The boat had stopped leaking!'

'Yes, thanks to the kind river god.'

'And the water which swelled the planks!'

'No, no, the most kind god.'

Grace said, 'Our Lord Jesus performed many miracles.' The women waited, but she said no more, having become discouraged.

Next day one of the women said, 'We all had the same dream every night. We all dreamt the river was a waterfall. It was because we were so frightened of the midstream. And then these two stupid old women went into midstream and were swept away and we had to chase for three days to rescue them.'

'You didn't care about us. You wanted the boat.'

'Yes, because you are old and useless. Anyway you lost the boat.' They fell silent, thinking how the two castaways had been found shivering on the bank down-river, their boat smashed and carried away.

'And when we came back our houses were full of drunks.'

'Three drunken men. They had slept in our houses and eaten all the dried fish. We drove them away with fish spears.'

'I cut one across the face. He will carry that scar for ever, and maybe I blinded him.'

They had eaten the watchdogs during their hunger, they said, and took turns sleeping among the boats. But they had dragged the boats further up the beach as they grew stronger, and in time could bring them to their proper places under the houses. They tied the prow ropes to their quilts and therefore had to sleep in their separate houses, though sometimes they had crept to each other in the middle of the night because they missed their families, or because they heard them breathing.

'Our husbands said that only a man can make water from a boat, but of course it's easy, provided you sit over the stern.'

'Life is good now.'

'Yes, the river god loves us and gives us lots of fish.'

'Even though we make water in his face.'

'We are the river's beautiful concubines.'

'No, his grandmothers and ugly old great-aunts.'

Grace said, 'But of course the one God is also the god of the river. And He is the god of the trees and mountains and everything. Really we should all pray to Him and honour only Him.'

The aunts only said, 'Life is good now.'

'We have lots of fish to cook, and leftovers to dry.'

'We don't weep now.'

'Except for our children.'

Here they fell silent, so Grace said, 'Your children are happy in heaven.' They didn't answer, so she said, 'I have no children. Perhaps one day I'll have children.'

'Yes, one day,' said the women.

'And your husband is not too old?' asked one. Grace explained that white hair is common among Western people.

'And the women also have white hair?' Grace assured her that some did.

'But your husband is too big,' said another, and the aunts laughed.

'And his white hair. Does he have white hair also . . .?' But here she was silenced by the others.

Next afternoon one of the women said, 'Men are useless. But they want to stay with us because we have a lot of fish.'

'They like the smell of old fish.'

'They gossip on the beach with us, but they look at the fish and count our boats and houses.'

'We send them away unfed.'

'Not always!' said one of the women.

'Yes, there is a young man here,' said another, a little embarrassed. 'Though he is at present in the hills.'

'But he is useless.'

'Fishermen make the best husbands,' said another, and again this seemed to be a joke.

'Men are afraid of us. Or they see the boats bouncing on the river and are afraid.'

'Or they see us with our knives, whish, whish.' And the woman jumped up and cleaned a fish with two passes of her knife, sharpened until it was narrow as grass, her laughter unbroken and the fish still flapping, though it was open as a book.

Grace said, 'I think it is wonderful that every fish is the same inside, so that we can see how God's handiwork is everywhere.'

'Men are useless,' said the woman with the knife. 'I don't need men.' But then the gutted fish was pushed down her trousers and her shrieks were very loud.

6

John loved the fishing, its art and tackle. He dreamt of Sho's boat in the push and swing of the current, and woke with a pleasant ache in his shoulders. The boat was stable as a raft, easier for John than the rolling canoe-like craft of the women, but the headman hated it and blamed his father.

Sho's father and uncle had worked for three years in a boatyard near the hardwood forests downstream, until they could bring the boat home like a bride, its ropes still yellow, fresh bruises on the keel where they had hauled it up the rapids. But then the criticism started. It was said that the boat's flat keel was cheap to make but only suited the smooth waters of the lowlands: in the rough upstream river it was clumsy like a raft of the tribals. The other men compared it with their own sharp keels, and Sho grew up ashamed of his father, who had been tricked and would soon drown.

His father didn't care, laughing with his brother in the mad boat and talking so often of the heyday of their youth – three years of earning and spending downstream – that when Sho left the beach he went upstream to test his strength rather than down to pamper his weakness. Yet after all the boat had caught him like a coffin.

It had always carried the fisher folk's heavier gear,

and Sho had added to the clutter as his courage failed. He and John fumbled among old baskets, fish spears and scoops, broken bamboo poles, tangles of rope, mats to cover the boat in the rain, a landing gaff with an iron barb, and a big net for the rare unpredictable shoals of fish, though the net was rotting because Sho never dried it over a smoky fire, even a fire in his house, which would also fumigate his walls and roof. He was afraid of the boat, bad as a young horse for an old man, and cursed its bamboo ropes, which were grey and fraying.

Sho wouldn't replace the ropes because they reminded him of an old bitterness. His father had learnt to make ropes at the downstream boatyard and thereafter relished his skill, splitting bamboo into straps, showing his son how the bamboo was turned inside out to make a cable – the hard outer parts plaited to make the tough core of the cable, the soft inner parts woven into its sheath. But bamboo warps and splits as it dries, won't take a nail, turns any blade, and cuts like razors, so headman Sho didn't follow his father's art, nor learn the knots which his father knew like good-luck characters, although he always stored the coiled ropes so that one end pointed upstream and the other down, making a path for the life energy – the *qi* – which flowed from the mountains to the sea and would otherwise collect in the rope, making it tangle and break.

His father had also tried to teach him the best fishing places. Fish travelled the river like men, and loved the bend for its slower waters. Resting here, they found boulders on the bottom: in their lee the current was even slower and was irresistible for the fish, until a boat was overhead and a spear stabbing. His father had steered to these boulders by stretching out an arm and aligning a finger and thumb on certain landmarks – the headland, a bush on the far bank – these landmarks and the choice of finger having been passed down through the generations, altered to suit the length of a fisherman's arm and the spread of his hand.

Sho's father had tried to show him these combinations of finger and thumb, and his uncle said that once he was married he would understand the river bottom, because it was like the funny places inside a wife. His father laughed at this, which was horrible since it recalled his mother. Sho trembled with anger and disgust when his father held out his crooked old fingers, so that all this fisher folk knowledge was lost.

He was afraid of the river, and was glad to fish with the white man, who had stopped discussing religion. John loved to pit his strength against the current pushing on the broad prow, where there was a tuft of feathers and ribbons which he told himself was only decoration. There was a wooden face in the stern, though, which was definitely the fish god.

John knew he should object to this totem, but liked the ugly wide-mouthed face laughing at them, and could see how fish might come to greet it and be caught.

In her journal Grace wrote: *This village is only five women, a little girl, and one man, or perhaps two. I see no hope of a successful Mission here. Mr Gerrard and I discussed the adjoining valley, with its opium plantation and riverboat port. He also suggested – with admirable optimism – that tribal people in the neighbouring hills will further augment the potential harvest of Souls.*

But I fear that, in allowing us to explore this place, the Imperial authorities have again demonstrated their fear of the Word. Instead I contemplate the larger settlements upriver, beyond this region of narrow gorges and meagre agriculture, even as far as Yunnan-fu, where so many cry out for news of the one Lord.

We were a little downcast and prayed for strength: then, invigorated by The Help Which Is Never Withheld, we resolved to do our best in the situation to which the Lord has brought us, but to communicate our doubts to the Mission, and to plan a journey upstream.

My husband said that this morning he had noticed a thing which we had both long anticipated: the air was so cool that his breath had been faintly visible, a phenomenon almost unknown to us natives of the sultry lower reaches of this river. I pondered for a few moments and then smilingly declared, 'May the words of the Lord become as visible to China's millions!'

The river water is brown and very cold. After a few hours, though, a fine dust lies in the bottom of the bucket and the water is clear. It makes delicious tea.

Grace's journal was her companion and consolation. She had been too uncomfortable to write during their trip to the pebble beach, and in any case was embarrassed under the immediate gaze of her husband, who seemed to agree with Ecclesiastes that 'of making many books there is no end; and much study is a weariness of the flesh'.

She thought, 'Like a book, John is bored by bookworms,' but did not tell her husband this joke, since she herself was perhaps a bookworm. Certainly it is written that 'the letter killeth, the Spirit giveth life,' but of course there is a paradox here – writing that says that writing doesn't signify. And indeed the Spirit is unreliable, drifting about like a cloud: how much surer if it is fixed with words, those black-headed nails.

So now she settled with pleasure in the last of the daylight to order her journal, which would one day be part of the library in Canton, informing the fresh recruits from Europe and America. She wrote how at Hong Kong harbour they had seen young French Catholic missionaries in Chinese clothes, their heads shaved to leave only a Chinese pigtail, so that the servants from the Mission declared them to be 'very number one Chinaman'.

Perhaps the French were a little too clever, as so often. She watched John tying fishing hooks, then wrote: *Does not this adopting of Chinese ways defeat the very purpose of coming to this country, which is to show the 'Celestial Empire' that other lands exist, and other customs as hallowed as its own?*

Then they had sailed south for three days to Haiphong, returning into China on the famous French railway. It was their first time on a real train and John had leant from the window, exclaiming at the bridges and tunnels while she held his hat, taking sly sniffs inside and laughing with him at the Chinese conductor who shrugged like a Frenchman. Then John sat down and she wiped the coal smuts from his face and settled the hat on his dear head, trying not to cry with happiness.

She hadn't noticed his unease. He had sat at the end of their bench and could stare along the corridor. It ran the length of the train so that he could see through to the coal tender. It was like a well or tunnel, except that it flexed with the railway line. There were many curves on the astonishing French railroad into China, but too often the corridor made a straight path for demons.

She wrote: *The British Consul at Sien-kiang was previously at Ssumao, whence he was driven by a mob crying, 'Kill, kill.' We had no desire to meet such a poor creature and merely told him of our coming in a brief note.*

We refreshed ourselves with tea from the picturesque little charcoal burner on the train, but on descending were at once surrounded by a crowd of local people, who had gathered outside the station when they heard what monsters were aboard. Most were eating as they followed us, and making raucous comments which I tried not to understand, except for the cries of 'Tortoise' and 'Rabbit' which are comical to us, though grave insults in China and which one must be careful not to find provoking.

As in Canton and Hong Kong, a great part of this crowd wore clothes woven in Lancashire of American cotton, even as they hooted at us. And hobbling at the outskirts of the crowd were two lepers, horribly deformed, begging for the white man's medicine, which

shows that at least some inland Chinese have an aware-
ness of what benefits might accrue from contact with the
'white demons'.

It is strange that such crowds should be apparent in
the railway towns, which are always described by visitors
as absolutely cosmopolitan and sophisticated: we won-
dered what scenes of ignorance and debasement might
await us in the hills.

At first they were reassured. They spent four days
on the famous Yunnan ponies, dazzled by the highland
paths and the mountains soaring around them, then
descending to villages which were announced by the smell
of excrement. After each day's journey of twenty-five or
thirty miles they slept at inns.

She would describe only the best of them: *The inn
was down three steps. The landlord wanted 300 chen,
double the normal price, which (as he correctly said) is
customary for any dealing with a foreigner. After my
husband's patient resistance, we paid little more than
a Chinese would, the price including four cups of rice, a
plate each of salt cabbage twice a day, a saucer of cotton
oil and a rush wick. Our hard bargaining is not from
material greed, of course, but because we are most conscious of the toil of our brothers and sisters in collecting
funds for our work, and because our modest capital –
equivalent to perhaps 200 American dollars – must serve
the Lord's purpose for a year.*

*Our bedroom was small, with one wall to the outside
and a paper window which let in the moonlight. On
either side, mat walls were all that screened us from the*

other guests, and we heard the whimpering of a child,
but fortunately it was soon stilled and we retired.

We had been well advised by the Mission and came
equipped with our own quilt and an oiled groundsheet to
spread over the bed. Nevertheless, within a few minutes
a hideous discomfort began. With cries of horror we rose
from the verminous bed, and spent the remainder of the
night on the rough planks of the floor.

Perhaps mentioning their shared bed was not seemly,
she thought. But it would be equally embarrassing to
delete the passage, as if ashamed of matrimony. Still, she
regretted that she had no pencil for a first draft.

Grace didn't describe what happened after they had
left their bed, though John would remember it always.
Feeling the insects still at work, they had slid from their
night clothes. She reached for her shift, but John stopped
her.

It was their first time together in this state, and their
bodies were strange to them. It was very warm, and they
were Adam and Eve in the moonlight. With a most tender
conversation they began their love-making, until waves
overwhelmed her. The hair creeping on his head, almost
unmanned, thinking of the listeners behind the mat walls,
John for the first time heard Grace's small cries, her face
Chinese with desire.

She had fallen asleep, exhausted by the tremendous
day, but John lay awake because he had seen the naked
engine of God's purpose, which binds husband and wife
so that new souls are formed to one day join Him in
heaven.

During the following days, when she couldn't write, she had indulged her favourite hobby: improving her knowledge of Chinese characters. The system was foolish, of course, clumsy as Roman numerals, but the little pictures were sometimes charming and therefore easy to learn: she recalled her delight as a child when shown that the character for peace was made of the character for woman under the character for roof.

On the final day of their journey she had noticed an amusing coincidence. She now wrote: *I was contemplating the good-luck characters painted around the door of a peasant's miserable hut, one of them being the character for happiness, which is written thus,* 福.

I wonder if any scholar has noticed that the four components of this ideogram are those for god, 示*, cultivated land,* 田*, first,* 一*, and mouth or person,* 口*. That night I pointed out to my husband that the makers of the Chinese alphabet precisely agreed with the authors of Genesis – that the epitome of happiness was the first person (Adam) with God in a garden. What a charming conceit this will make for the recruiting of Chinese converts!*

At last, from the crest of a little cliff, we gazed with emotion on the rushing waters of the great river. How touching it was to see again our childhood friend, and to think that the very waters we now gaze upon will, after who knows how many weeks, and after how many strange sights and unknown scenes, pass our childhood homes – Canton, where my dear Mr Gerrard took his first faltering steps, and then, as it melts into the ocean, my own sea-girt Hong Kong.

Nevertheless we are struck by its transformation. In the great estuary which was our home, the river is a serene old gentleman moving with composure to his dissolution. But here the headlong torrent is a brutal youth, who has a man's strength but not his courtesy.

They rode upstream, following a rocky track along the bank, Grace relieved that their overland journey was ending: she had felt responsible for China, she decided, and ashamed that her husband should see its failings. Yet he was so friendly and calm, thinking that nothing could reach him, while she was down in the mill of the crowded Chinese.

His silences worried her, and inclined her to talk. She wrote: *I reminded my husband how the character for man is 人, derived from what was once the sketch of a striding figure. I then repeated to him the famous (though perhaps impious) line of King Lear: 'Man is no more but such a poor, bare, forked animal,' and explained how, with reference to Chinese script, one might punningly replace the word 'animal' with 'ideogram'!*

My husband did not reply, since at that moment we were rounding a bend in the riverbank. He stared with deep curiosity at a tiny settlement ahead of us. After a few moments I too fell silent, because this would be our new home.

That night, while Grace wrote, a young man slipped back to the village. His name was Jivu Lanu and he was a shaman with three spirit servants – a wolf, a snake, and a crocodile, the latter being the most powerful. They had previously been familiars of his father, also a shaman, who had been murdered before Jivu was born. They had come to Jivu while he worked as a porter, having waited in the ghost world until he came of age, and for the rest of that day he could carry two sacks of grain, which only one other man in the valley could do. Since then, however, they had often left him in times of difficulty so that he believed they would punish and preserve him until his father was avenged.

Now Jivu lived by selling medicines, breaking evil spells, bottling demons, making charms from the scrotum sacs of buffaloes, and lying entranced while his spirit travelled to the land of the dead to reclaim those who were gripped by a fever, though he was not wholehearted in this latter skill, which seemed undignified.

But it was a weary life, every village the same, the women with their complaints, the men mocking his visions but listening when he talked to the gods of the game animals or, in quiet corners, sold them herbs for potency. Only after he had raised a false irritation could he summon the energy to perform: he would scowl at the villagers, feeling the wolf in him, so that they wondered at his bad temper. He had a silver snake, thin as a twig, which slid in through his nose and out through his mouth, but it had lately died.

He came from the upper reaches of the river, and had never travelled so far downstream, where the water was dirty. The aunts had a curiosity for anyone who had grown up near the headwaters, so he was given food. He sat cross-legged on the pebble beach, telling his stories in good Mandarin or bad Cantonese, but his youth told against him: they asked about the river and the habits of fish, but his answers were unconvincing. Flustered, he declared that his crocodile spirit spent much time in the water, but the aunts laughed and instead talked about themselves: they were nearly forty and accumulating disorders.

At this he had opened his wonderful pack, which was a wooden box as square as a cupboard, with shelves and drawers full of paper packages, bamboo cylinders plugged with wood or paper, and bottles made of leather, glass or pottery. He revealed some of their contents: wood from a tree struck by lightning, which cured fevers and the fear of fire; wood from the east-extending branch of a pear tree; ashes of wood from an old privy; a balm made of peppermint and black plum; extract of baby urine; fungus from the inside of a coffin; mouldy bean curd for sore throats; a speck of amber which was the petrified soul of a tiger; tiger bones which were only ox bones darkened with smoke.

The aunts were impressed but said nothing, being cunning negotiators. For the moment they took his less expensive charms, made from mountain herbs, which they tied to their boats and the eaves of their houses. They did not pay him, reasoning that he was compensated by their hospitality. Discontented, Jivu had left to search the hills for medicinal plants, and had spent several profitable days in a village which had never seen such a youthful shaman.

Now, around the fire on the pebble beach, the aunts

warned him about the white giant, whose hands were like fishing scoops. Jivu was startled to find missionaries in this obscure country, but said that three whites from Yunnan-fu had come to a village upriver and handed out leaflets, which he had thrown to the ground and beaten like snakes, and that he had been warned of their coming by his spirits and had walked for eight days and nights, only stopping to weave new shoes: he had destroyed three pairs on his journey.

And he revealed that while he had been stamping on the leaflets, his wolf spirit – which, although the most junior, was in many ways the most useful – had wrestled with Jesus in the ghost world, pulling his red hair and stealing his shiny black boots. Jivu stamped with a frown around the fire, puffing his cheeks, spreading his arms and walking with open legs, which showed that he too could be big when possessed. No doubt his spirits had led him to the fisher folk village, he said, to beat the missionaries again.

But Jivu was lying. He had come to the village to resolve his father's murder.

7

'We must leave this place,' said Grace. 'Though I know you love your fishing.'

They were sitting on the beach. Somewhere a child was crying. For a week the catches had been good, so the aunts had set aside this day for dressing their haul: they would sell the fish in Market Village. Headman Sho ignored such women's work and stayed indoors with his wife, though he would lead the aunts to the market and take possession of the cash, which they needed for the collector's fishing tax and to buy steel hooks and silk fishing line.

John was bent over Sho's upturned boat. Reluctantly he said, 'What should we do?'

'We can either write to your foolish Mr Burkett and ask permission to move upriver, or simply inform him that we have left: I favour the latter.' She added, 'Why is that child crying? It must be little Shen.'

John was mending the boat's leaky keel. The boat-yards shaped wood with an axe, so that every boatman on the river carried split bamboo to plug the gaps between his ragged planks. But Sho's boat stamped the water like a boot in a puddle, so that its flat keel flexed and the bamboo caulks were lost. That morning, on an impulse, John had hurried to the riverport at Market

Village and bought proper caulking paste at the storehouse. It was made of hemp, tung oil and lime and should flex and hold.

It was hard to think, though, because of the crying child. It could only be Shen, the headman's daughter, but he didn't understand why the fisher folk ignored her. He stood up, wiping his hands, and walked down the line of stilted huts along the beach. Under them was a gross litter, waiting to be purged by the next flood. He slithered on rocks green with fish slime.

He saw movement among the rubbish, and watched closely: the rats here were huge. But it was Shen. She lay among the filth, a greasy cloth over her slumped head.

'No, it is not our child,' cried the headman's wife, leaning from her door. 'It is only A'Hut.'

The name meant 'the beggar', and John bent in bewilderment over the child. For a moment he doubted his eyes. Was it not little Shen?

'It is a beggar child!' shrieked the woman. 'Nobody wants her.'

The child had soiled herself, yet was otherwise clean under the ostentatious rags. He lifted the infant and carried her, light as a pillow, up the rickety ladder to the house.

As he approached, the woman clasped her hands to her breast, her eyes fixed on the little bundle. John lifted the child towards her and saw how she yearned to grasp it. Inside the little house, the altar had fresh coloured paper and an oil lamp burning, and no sign of Shen. Now he was sure.

The headman's wife loved her daughter but was terrified of the demon which tormented her with sickness. She had cast copper coins on to the beach, which even the older women had been frightened to take, and had drawn on scraps of paper until they looked like money, burning them in front of the altar, hoping the demon would be satisfied with these riches instead of sickening little Shen.

But most of all she had spurned the infant. 'Beggar!' she whispered through her tears. 'Go! Why do you stay?'

Demons like torturing a treasured child, but get no pleasure from an orphan. So her mother had crouched before the altar, beating her head on the cane floor, offering tea, cakes, fruit and other dainties, but had never specified the reason for her fears, lest the demon overhear. At last she had carried Shen from the house and clad her in dirt, which demons hate, being clean as cats.

John examined the little bundle for typhoid, which was the black killer of country folk. It was only diarrhoea, so he said, 'Yes, it is a beggar child. I'll take it to my house to be a slave.'

Grace prescribed the latest treatment – the water from boiled rice, with sugar and a pinch of salt – but the case was not serious, so that they wondered about her mother, who could abandon the child for no reason. After a day or two the infant began to totter around the house with a pale face and bruised eyes, or sat on John's knee, watching him with adoration. Her parents came but didn't touch her. Nor did they wish John and Grace to show affection, in case the demon renewed its torments.

When Grace couldn't hear, John whispered, 'Beggar child, whom nobody wants.'

Grace wrote: *Shen has the sad old eyes of many peasant children, but – within these limits – has again become mischievous, resuming a kind of heavy gaiety, her bright smile disconcerting under those shadowed eyes. Today, with great ceremony, we took her home, the outward and visible sign of our success being that her name is once more spoken aloud. For the first time I entered a hovel of the fisher folk and saw the pitifully bare conditions in which they live, the only ostentation, almost the only colour, being the decorations for the small altar to their fish god which occupies one corner. As I said later to my husband, this devotion to their heathen deity can be taken as perversely encouraging, being an augury of their faithfulness to Christianity.*

The father of this poor infant is the village head-man. His possession of a 'useless' girl is proof enough of his comfortable position, and, I would like to feel, of an essential goodness, since in many poor villages there are only sons, especially where running water is so close.

During our visit the headman complained of the impositions of Yue Fat, whom he accused of inventing new taxes. Like many of the more ignorant men of China, he will not address a woman directly: instead he answered via my husband, or looked at the wall and spoke in generalities, so that, when I asked if Yue was greedy, he addressed the door frame with a lofty discourse to the effect that: 'Many of the mandarin type look to their own advantage.'

He seemed doubtful of the hysterical superstitions of his wife, who is a poor trembling thing, although pretty, and seems half distracted, or is perhaps a mental defective, a state which is so common in these hills, thanks to inadequate nutrition, though one would not expect it among those with access to the river's riches. The headman, instead, merely accedes to his wife's desires, which – though apparently cruel – were caused only by concern for her child. So this is an opportunity which might be called Heaven-sent, except that Heaven would never contemplate such torture of an infant.

The smell of fish is everywhere.

The headman's wife was called Little Niece. When cholera killed half the village she had been unmarried and almost young enough to die with the children. Indeed she had wished to follow her parents and brothers, whose bodies had gone into the river and been carried far downstream to the underworld.

After their deaths Little Niece would not go into her family house, instead sleeping with her arms around one of the four older women and waking her with dreams of drowning. A cormorant began fishing from the roof of her empty house, and the women declared that its bad fortune must have left. Little Niece said that cormorants had perched on the houses before the watery sickness and so meant nothing. Then the women showed her where a small bird had woven a nest in her straw walls. Little Niece agreed that she would go home when the nestlings had flown. That night one of the women threw the nestlings into the river and next day helped her to move back.

In the sad house she remembered her dead brothers and her young dead parents. The house creaked with their comings, but their faces grew blurred in her recollection, which was due to the smoothing action of the river, her parents in particular becoming smoothed and youthful until they could watch from among their dead children.

She had been spoiled as a child. When she was young like little Shen, her father had painted good-luck characters on the back of her hands so that he would know if she had played in the forbidden water. Once, as she crouched over a game on the beach, a gourd sewn on her coat so that she would not drown, he had snatched her up and rowed her out onto the shallows, his brother grumbling about the uncleanness of females. Then he had sons, who went out every day: they too wore a gourd, and were tied on a rope fastened to the prow, and wore a bell whose silence would mean they had fallen in the river. But Little Niece could no longer touch the boat in case her blood should come.

She had grown up feeling that she could follow her small concerns while others protected her: but after the watery demon killed her family she kept to her circle out of fear. She watched the older women learning to row, but stayed on land, catching crabs on the river bank with a baited line, drawing them in so softly that more crabs attacked the first and were still fighting when they were dropped into the pot which boiled all day over the driftwood fire. Their slimy meat was only fit for geese and ducks, and no one would eat it but Little Niece, who lost herself in picking bits from the shells. Her instinct was to hoard, to hide, to be silent.

She felt nothing when the headman chose her for a wife. She hadn't encouraged him, but knew in her vague way that she was the prettiest. The headman liked this vagueness, and tumbled her backwards while her eyes were dizzy and her fingers were blind as roots of vegetables. He was proud of the squeaking of their hut, which the other women would hear, and of the eagerness of his young wife, who bounced beneath him like his flat-bottomed boat. After Shen was born Little Niece grew discouraged in their lovemaking because the headman didn't touch that part which the fisher folk called 'a man in a boat'.

Instead she recalled her family. The headman saw these recollections as an insult, and said she neglected their daughter. But Little Niece loved Shen and sometimes held her hard because children slip through your fingers like water, although the harder you hold them the more they slip away. It was just that she had so many distractions – paddling in the shallows among her mother's whispers and kisses, or dreaming that a fishing line was around her throat, or that her father rebuked her and called to her from downstream, or that her net was full of dead children and would drag her under. Indeed, to live by the river was wearying because it dragged like a full net, pulling you downstream to the underworld and its ghosts.

On good days she walked in the shallows, baby Shen strapped between her breasts, throwing her net gracefully but not far, enjoying the current between her pretty legs, which wavered under her and grew numb in the awful cold, which was the beginning of melting. Little Niece knew that she had hardly enough bones to resist the river, having too much of its waters within her.

There were few fish in the shallows so she caught only enough for a meal and didn't share them, pulling the net to shore with its tiny catch and eating everything with little Shen, even the smallest transparent fingerlings which normally pass through the net and which she should have thrown back. Her favourite was the white-rice fish, which is transparent when caught but white as macaroni when boiled, and she sucked off its flesh in a mouth so soft and will-less that the bones didn't prick. She disliked slices from the larger fish.

Shen grew big enough to be left on the beach, so Little Niece went deeper into the river. She would not mind drowning, she felt, and because of this had found the still spot. Even now it took a leap of faith to wade there, because the water was up to her breast and very fast before the river ceased to deepen and her bare feet were climbing a bank of cold sand. The water at the still spot came to her waist, which was too deep for comfort, but the current was so slow that leaves and dead insects floated there, and occasional driftwood which she took for the fire.

Recently Little Niece had spent more time at the still spot: during the day, when everyone was fishing, she was

73

alone on the beach with the white woman and the young shaman. If they came close she left little Shen and fled into the river, where only the aunts came drifting by.

The aunts remembered that their husbands had talked about a certain spot in the river, calling it by the slang name for a woman's private organ. After long thought they decided that the river must curl back on itself in the lee of the bend, and that the still spot was the centre of this turning, where the water was slow enough to drop its silt, and little fish needn't fight the current and could eat the small things that fish find in silt. The aunts saw how, being a favourite of the fish, it had been a favourite of their dead menfolk, whose boats must have hung there without effort and with many productive casts of their nets.

They smiled crookedly to see Little Niece so proud in the middle of the river. She should stop worrying about her dead family, they agreed: she was mad out of vanity, and vain because she was pretty.

Then the watery demon returned and seized little Shen. Jivu Lanu said that the child should be abused and ignored, but the white people saved her. Thereafter Little Niece came close when the aunts talked to the white woman around the driftwood fire: like Grace, the aunts believed in a father god, but would not abandon their lesser gods, as Grace required. Little Niece said nothing, but loitered outside their circle, listening with her face turned away, learning that the dead didn't go to a cold darkness but to the Christian heaven, which was warm and bright.

One morning, when John was leaving her house after the ritual at the altar, she said quietly, 'You come from downriver. My family went there. Tell me about my family.'

John was embarrassed: headman Sho was watching from the ladder, and Little Niece stood too close. 'Your family is with God,' he said. 'They are happy that you have a child and a good husband.'

Little Niece had thought that her dead family was cold and hungry, so that she must light lamps and burn offerings. Now in her doubt she let the lamps run dry and delayed the gifts of paper money, angering her husband because his own spirit might likewise be neglected.

As the aunts tended their shrines they thought, 'Certainly this barbarian religion would save lamp oil.' Otherwise they were not much interested in Christianity, which had nothing to say about rivers.

8

Grace and John were climbing the steep slope behind their house. They wanted to see the valley over the ridge, where there might be a harvest of souls among the opium masters and their slaves, though Grace was doubtful.

They called on the way at the house of the collector Yue Fat. The young private, his arms bare and black, was making coal bricks in the yard at the house side. He shouted something and two older men poked their heads around the door of their shed, their faces slack with boredom. There were hurried mutterings and they emerged strapping on their shoulder armour of cloth-covered bamboo. One was a middle-aged corporal, who Grace and John hadn't seen before. He pushed past them, rather rudely perhaps, and went inside.

While they waited, the sergeant, old and shrivelled, stood extravagantly on guard, though John was diverted by his musket, an ancient Imperial matchlock. John had seen such weapons used by farmers in the fens around Canton, their long barrels betokening bad gunpowder, but they hadn't been army issue for twenty years. And the smouldering cord which fired it was tucked unlit in the soldier's belt.

Perhaps it was early for the little secretary. They waited while the young soldier mixed the coal dust and clay and his comrades scowled, and John noted how the house was little different from their own, though better appointed: perhaps it was the pattern for wooden houses in these parts. Finally the dapper little man emerged, sleepy and smiling and speaking English: 'You are welcome. Thank you, thank you.'

That night Grace wrote: *At the time of our first encounter with the Collector, Mr Gerrard and I had not unpacked, so now I gave the secretary our papers, which comprised a consular passport declaring my husband to be a foreign 'sz-foo' or 'scholar', travelling with his wife. The Celestial gentleman expressed the usual bewilderment at such an insignificant scrap of paper. There is a vain and foolish tradition in China that official documents must be large, their size being a measure of importance. I do wonder whether it might not be wise for our own documents to be larger, thus giving them a proper dignity.*

It seems that the cheerful informality of our visit was too vulgar for the refined sensibilities of a Mandarin, for we were not invited to penetrate his splendid solitude, even though that gentleman had been received with Christian good fellowship during his impromptu – and uninvited – visit to our own house, and even though we carried the gift of a bar of soap, bought in Hong Kong for my own use but found to be unsuitable, being scented.

Instead we were guided from the zone of his estimable presence by the little secretary, who remembered our plan to visit the plantation and was determined to accompany us. With many expressions of superficial friendliness he walked with us up the slope, which rapidly levelled out, even becoming a kind of meadow, although the ground is perhaps too stony for agriculture.

For the first time the secretary told us his name, which is Chang, and seemed almost mockingly genial, perhaps knowing that he was intruding. But my husband is an expert at benign resistance, and the little man's smiles became uncertain. What a passionate creature he is! Really there is something childish about him, so violently changing from cheeriness to a schoolgirl sulk.

We crossed the stony field, the air perceptibly cooler, and the secretary turning to look back to the valley. It was a most impressive sight, although the river by now was hidden below the slope.

The secretary gave his meaningless laugh and said, 'We should go back. Time for more tea. And (with a little bow to me) we have some of the sweets you liked.'

'Oh, but we must continue,' said Mr Gerrard, with a far larger and more genuine smile. At this the little man – who seemed quite a child beside my mighty husband – was downcast, perhaps because he wore the foolish cloth shoes so common among all classes of Chinese, the only distinction being their degree of decoration, although many have no footwear at all, of course.

Mr Gerrard and I were well shod in stout black leather and had no qualms about scaling the loftiest peak, let alone the slope which lay in our path. I was disappointed to find the little creature determined to continue with us, though my impatience was cooled at the sight of his helpless struggles with the rocky slope.

I suppose he is the kind of precious young man who has climbed nothing more arduous than a sedan chair (which I like to call a 'sit-down' chair!), but even my husband, so strong and tall, was breathless, and we stopped several times to admire the widening view.

At last we reached the summit of the ridge, where a remarkable prospect of fearsome valleys and rocky hill-tops was spread before our gaze, including snowy peaks in the distance towards Thibet. With the land of the Lord's promise spread before us, I dared to recall Moses on Pisgah, though my pride would soon receive its remedy.

For several minutes I stood in awe, the little secretary growing restless, which quite distracted Mr Gerrard and me from proper appreciation of the tremendous vista, and of the Mighty Hand which fashioned it. I then recalled that 'he that observeth the wind shall not sow; and he that regardeth the clouds shall not reap', and therefore turned away, instead telling Chang of my game with the character for happiness, and suggesting that it might impress new converts to Christianity.

The secretary laughed but did not answer. We 'old China hands' have an adage that 'In China the ignorant believe in everything and the educated in nothing,' and I concluded that Chang will not be among the early converts to the one true God! On the contrary, I will use him as a kind of backwards compass, believing that anything which worries him must advance our work.

Now his steps lagged like those of a stubborn child, yet we insisted on crossing the ridge to the far side, where we hoped to see more of our harvest, the local tribal peoples. Here the Chinaman tried another of his unwise essays into English, but Mr Gerrard and I quite failed to understand. He said, 'I will be your . . .' but there followed a remarkable confusion of the sounds r and l and p and b, and we asked again and again for a repetition, provoking the little man to ever greater stammering, embarrassment and irritation – and consequently to our own ever greater bewilderment.

At last we understood him to say: 'I will be your interpreter.'

However, I have since maintained that Chang's promise was in fact: 'I will be your interrupter.' How we have laughed at this apt confusion, and the destruction of the man's silly pride!

And I have told my husband, 'Secretary Chang is a small man who stands on his dignity. Or, we might say, who stands on ceremony!'

We had already seen, during our first journey to the Mission House, the crop of the next valley. Sure enough, from our vantage point on the ridge, we again looked on great fields of opium – so heavily suppressed around the coastal regions, yet here blatantly in view. Since our arrival the first blooms of the poppies have opened in pink and white, or in the sultry crimson of popular imagining.

The secretary said that most of the plantation workers were of the Miao people, and working off a debt, thus substituting useful labour for their habitual drunkenness and war. Having read of such 'debt slavery' I have not the slightest doubt that these poor creatures have no hope *of liberty this side of the grave, and that their children and grandchildren will live and die in bondage in a futile attempt to repay their obligations. Again pride entrapped me as I recalled the Lord's injunction to all missionaries: 'I send thee, to open their eyes, and to turn them from darkness to light, and from the power of Satan unto God.'*

The secretary was by now become wearisome, and we scarcely glanced at him as we descended a narrow track towards the opium fields on the valley bottom. He in turn made no pretence of cheerfulness, and declared that he would wait for us on the valley side. We felt his gaze, not especially friendly, as we completed our journey down the slope and came to a raised track which ran up the middle of the valley, our passage attracting the open-mouthed gaze of the labourers in the fields on either side, until the crack of an overseer's whip returned them to their toil.

Thanks to slavery, human labour is hereabouts cheaper than that of animals. Nevertheless there was one buffalo, and its appearance prompted a curious obser-vation. As with so many of its fellows in China, the horns of this creature curve backwards over its neck, their sharp tips turning inwards to make a shape like an antique lyre. Such an arrangement prevents the creature from goring its keepers: in the wild, of course, it is equally incon-venient. It follows that all such animals are descended from some single individual, a sport of nature which its human keepers chose as progenitor of half the buffalo of Asia. It occurred to me that brothers and sisters reading

*this account might use this exemplar in their preaching,
to show how the Lord will not grossly intervene in the
world, but will send aid which we might, with the wit
that He also supplies, adapt to our advantage.*

*How we were touched to see these slaves toil in misery
for want of the Good News of salvation! I recalled the
holy words: 'We were Pharaoh's bondmen in Egypt; and
the Lord brought us out of Egypt with a mighty hand.'
And I thought how the misery of slaves is shared by
those who oppress them, who are enslaved in ignorance,
and must likewise be freed.*

*Yet, even as I was filled with compassion, my hopes
were rudely dashed!*

*As we walked towards the settlement called Market
Village, which is only a few houses for the slaves and
their masters and a mooring place for the riverboat, I
grew conscious of our isolation in the bottom of this
valley. Now we were approached by a group of slaves
and overseers, in all perhaps thirty persons. My husband saluted them in Cantonese, but they replied with
the most violent insults.*

*Under the assault of their harsh words and occasional
blows, including a cut to my husband's ankle from an
overseer's whip, we retreated whence we had come.
Stones and cries pursued us, many delivered by the slaves
we had come to comfort, and I was much disturbed by
the hideous dogs of the overseers, which howled and
snarled, encouraged by their masters as we hurried back
up the ridge.*

Yet most provoking of all, perhaps, was the expres-

sion on the face of the little secretary, which was such that I suspect a conspiracy, and a well-laid preparation for our visit to the plantation, although my husband reserves his judgement.

Returning to the collector's house, maintaining as best we could the courage appropriate to our calling, my brave husband refusing to limp despite the blood on his trousers, we heard the beating of a gong, which we discovered was in the hands of the collector's elderly sergeant. As we approached he grinned broadly. Although the gong was intended to call back the secretary, yet the soldier continued insolently to beat it, and to grin at us, his wizened old face recalling the shrunken heads kept as trophies by Borneo cannibals. As a gong is used to drive away devils, so this shrivelled old man wished to drive off the barbarians.

Because of this, we turned our steps to our more modest habitation, where our wounds could be tended in privacy, free of the (I am convinced) gloating attentions of Secretary Chang. Nevertheless, the gong was audible inside our house, so that I was indignant at the affront to everyone who feels called to 'preach Him among the heathen'.

China is both arrogant and wrong, and the decline of its greatness belies its complacency. This is the country which, a thousand years ago, invented paper money – the very sign and signal of an ordered nation – but where the currency is now copper coins and the so-called 'dollar', whose value is no more than the metal content, so that the system is merely an elevated form of barter.

So whence comes this addle-headed superiority, when one is everywhere surrounded by decay and the wreck of empire, its battlements crumbling, its paved roads rutted, the stones cut in the days of its greatness taken for pig sties!

I take up my pen again to note that the youngest of the collector's soldiers has brought a message from his master, one which – in my present humour – seems a further insult: we are invited to dinner.

9

The shaman Jivu Lanu liked the fisher folk village. His belly was full, and he felt the summer coming and the cool breeze from the river. Even the smell of fish had ceased to trouble him. 'All villages smell,' he thought. His throat tightened against the drinking water, however, which was full of swillings from upstream.

At night he curled on the floor of one hut or another, according to the whim of his demons, but had disappointed the aunts. Impatient, they asked him to come fishing, saying they needed magic. But he knew they only wanted his labour, and instead he lay all day on the floor of a hut, his chin on the threshold, staring at Grace on the beach or Little Niece in the shallows. He was tall for a native and very thin.

Sometimes Grace passed nearby with her water bucket, and he called the Cantonese greeting, 'Have you eaten?' She frowned and ignored him, sensing a mockery, but at last she paused below the hut and said, 'God's blessing on you. I come with a message from the only God.'

'Tell me your message.'

'That God loves you and wants you to love Him.'

'I don't love your God.'

'Perhaps you don't know Him.'

'Your God is a god for the white men,' said Jivu. 'I have my own gods, as do all the people of China.'

'China has little gods. Gods of the river, of the mountains, the god in a tree. But I come with news of the chief and only God, who made the world and loves what He has made.'

'Let your God, who loves me, give me money.'

'He won't be ordered,' said Grace.

'I don't order Him. I ask Him for money.'

It was uncomfortable to stare up, so Grace laid a hand on the bamboo ladder. But Jivu snatched it up to the doorway and laughed. 'Let your God lift you up.'

'Or perhaps He will lift you down,' said Grace. But the shaman began to dance and sing in the doorway, swinging the ladder until she left.

It was exciting to humiliate a woman, especially one so rich and pale, and he thought how she might have come up the ladder to him. Then he was ashamed. He had come to the village with a clear purpose, but had grown comfortable. He must proceed, before these white demons spoiled his plan.

Grace had pinned three posters to the wooden walls of the sitting room: one was of the Good Samaritan, one of the Prodigal Son and another of the crown of thorns with the text 'The Lord hath laid on Him the iniquity of us all'. But the aunts evaded all invitations, so she continued her discussions on the beach, accompanied by the pail of milled rice, which was a great luxury and caused many exclamations as to the whiteness and plumpness of the grains, which the aunts mixed with flaked fish and hot spices and shared with her.

She told the aunts that Jesus loved them – a thing unknown in their cosmology, in which a spirit was good if it might for a moment be placated. She said that this was news of great joy, but the aunts secretly agreed that it was easy to be happy when you were young, and to think you were happy because you were wise. Then they saw that Grace wasn't happy, because of John's fishing.

As she sat on the beach or studied on her veranda she often glanced at the river, hoping his boat might be back in the shallows, but seeing it by the far bank, half-hidden among the waves like a coffin carried shoulder-high. She saw the fisher folk stabbing to the bottom of the river with their spears, and hated the water for being as deep as a man is tall. It meant that the river was like a hurrying crowd. She thought of John pitched into these pilgrims, shouting as he was bustled away.

Already frightened, she became incredulous – John was venturing out alone. At first he stayed in the calm behind the bend, practising his rowing. He loved to stand with the long oars crossed at his chest, leaning forward until the boat made foam on the flat water. But then she watched appalled as he crabbed sideways to the far bank, dropping the prow rope over the mooring pole as the great rock raced past.

She said he had forgotten his mission, but he didn't answer, thinking that the Western way of rowing was stupid: boatmen here could lean their whole weight on the oars and could see where they were going. She hated these silences, which seemed like anger. She said, 'You are terrible as an army with bunions,' but he didn't smile.

A few days earlier she had written: *How interesting is the word 'fluent'; so often used to describe speech but derived, I presume, from 'like a river'.*

But now the river had stolen her husband, so she noted: *It is sometimes said that China, Egypt and Mesopotamia were the first to be civilised because their people must band together to tame great rivers: government grew from irrigation and flood control. By that argument, the wildness of this place derives from its untameable river. Instead of the sweet arts of conversation we have the roar of water: instead of civilisation we have its immoderate rage!*

John was launching the boat one morning when the headman's wife appeared. Perhaps she was embarrassed, because she conveyed her desire with gestures and nods. But her intention was clear, although surprising, and he helped her into the boat. Her hand was dry and hard like the pads of a dog.

She gripped the gunwales as the boat crabbed across the river to the far side, then bounced on the waves behind the tethering rock, water spurting from under the keel. But the white giant was tall as a father, and she felt safe.

Grace had been sitting on the veranda, absorbed in her study of Chinese characters and sometimes looking upstream, thinking how the river reached its fingertips towards Tibet. Beyond was India and the Holy Land:

from there the sons of Noah had repopulated the earth, spreading also into China. Then she saw John and Little Niece.

That evening she said nervously, 'The headman's wife is pretty as a picture, but almost as silent. It is the tragedy of our sex that men can judge such silence as achievement enough.'

John was silent, but remembered how he had only talked to Little Niece about the dead in heaven, who live in contentment with the Lord. That night he dreamt that Little Niece said, 'To swim in the water we must be bare as the water,' which seemed a great truth and silenced his theology.

Grace never again watched him on the river, hastening her plans for a move upstream.

Jivu Lanu had also seen the white man with Little Niece. Jealous, he told the aunts that she was the source of their ill-luck, as evidenced by her madness and her sickly child. That night around the driftwood fire he questioned them about domestic animals. Greatly excited, he learnt that they had eaten the watchdogs.

'This is how Little Niece was possessed!' he said. Animals which live close to humans – namely dogs, cats, rabbits, horses, donkeys, and mules – often become a home for hungry ghosts, he said. Such animals should never be eaten by a woman, except of course if there is a wise shaman who can perform the correct ceremony, because the ghost will occupy her womb and bring miscarriages, deformities, and infant deaths.

A hungry ghost, resident in the watchdog, had surely killed their families with the watery sickness, said Jivu. When the dog was eaten it had moved to Little Niece, had made her mad and sickened her child, had driven away suitors for the aunts, and had brought the white barbarians and the greedy collector. An exorcism was needed.

The aunts knew that shamans always see hungry ghosts, just as healers see disease. But they didn't object: exorcisms were enjoyable, and Jivu Lanu couldn't expect much payment since he'd been fed and housed for so long.

Jivu didn't mention his deepest fear: that the ghost inside Little Niece was that of his father. How horrible that he had desired her. He was still punished with celibacy, and would not be free until he had exorcized his murdered father and had punished the chief murderer – headman Sho.

10

When Sho was young there were plenty of men and children in the village. Indeed it was so populous that the fish god couldn't supply enough fish. Amongst the children were five boys, including Sho: they were the pride of the village, but grew up believing that hunger was a natural state.

When they were older they explored upriver and found a side stream with fish that were big enough to drag a man in. They stood on a midstream rock to catch them, but the rock was smaller than the fish so the youngsters ran a rope from their belt to a tree, and took turns to work alone with a spear and line, a joss-stick burning as a timer.

In the evenings they took the fish back to the village, though their parents were angry because the upstream tribes were famous for cruelty. One of Sho's friends was shot with a poison dart and henceforward limped, but they continued their expeditions, dressed in ribbons and bright feathers.

They grew sleek and glossy and the old headman, who the boys mocked, decided they were not returning with all their fish, but that he would not confront them. His wife said that her husband should go with the youngsters, though perhaps they would walk too fast for him. These comments were made in the presence of the five young men, who laughed.

The headman burned offerings to bring fish to the village, but his wife also sneered at this: indeed it was a womanly activity. He felt undermined, and remembered how he had taken the village from the previous headman, who now pottered under the houses or helped the women with their washing, smiling at everyone.

By now the young men were travelling each day to the limits of what was tolerable. One day, at their favourite fishing spot, they cut the large leaves of a sappy plant and made a shelter against a summer storm. But the rain didn't stop, so they stayed all night. They ate much of their catch and had to fish again in the morning. That afternoon they reluctantly started home. On their next trip they brought blankets.

They built a hut further up the bank. It was exciting to sleep in a house on the ground, with a delicious fear of snakes. After a night of singing and laughter they would sleep late: then, draped in coloured feathers, they would climb down over mossy boulders to their separate fishing spots, shouting to each other up the echoing valley and at last noticing young women watching from the bushes. They were daughters of the local tribe, a branch of the Yi people: there were many taboos about the river so the girls admired these bold young strangers.

The boys still took fish to their families, though they never all came together: someone must guard their camp, they explained. They boasted about the fish, which were plentiful and stupid, and how they had taken beautiful wives from the local tribe, which would therefore not trouble them. They didn't bring their wives, however, who would have seen the tall houses and curving boats and would have wished to stay.

They presented their fish with formality, like a gift from one settlement to another, but their parents turned away: they would not accept the fish as if they were the payment of a debt, and the boys had to lay the fish on the ground. Their parents were desolated by the loss of their sons, and foresaw a hungry future in a village of old people and infants. In a rage they said that a son should bring his wife to his home village, and not leave like a daughter. The boys were irritated: they had carried the fish all day.

In return the five young men wanted rods and spears and nets, but their families proved fierce. The arguments became bitter, and a net was torn when Sho argued with his father. The young men didn't consider the less interesting equipment, and therefore started their settlement with no axe or mattock and nothing to hold water. Their village took years to build, and the laziest of them, who still limped from the poison dart, lived alone in a shelter hardly bigger than himself, pushing into the other huts when the rain was bad: he had been fat, but grew lean and grey and acquired ulcers. He continued to sing and make whistles but looked so old that the children believed he had much wisdom.

He was the last to stop fishing. Their catches had shrunk even before they were properly settled, but no one could face another move. He laid traps in the shallows but checked them rarely: they were always empty or were smashed by the tribes. He thought about the fish god, that creature of their childhood, who might be angry at their fishing and perhaps had withdrawn his army. Later, as his own troubles grew, he saw that the god was grieving at the bottom of the river because his soldier sons were dead.

His friends had long since turned to the land. It was steep and covered with ferns, mossy boulders, and dripping overhangs. The sun hit it aslant. The rainy season wasn't longer than elsewhere, but all year its tepid waters trickled from porous rocks above their fields, washing out the goodness. They ate snails, the bitter tips of bracken, and a kind of small frog, which they called 'field chicken', which half swam and half clambered through the moss.

They were too weary to move, and dared not hunt because the tribes would surely kill them. Their bright feathers grew mouldy on the walls of their damp huts, and their women were bent-backed from carrying soil. Travelling healers and sellers of tobacco and salt didn't climb to visit them, but the tribes took shortcuts across their land.

At night around their single fire they said they should go back to fishing, but the wives grew indignant and recited the tribal taboos, which their husbands had been punished for ignoring. In any case their gear was worn out or turned to other purposes – the nets used for sacks, the hooks dissolved into rust like a curl of hair, and the biggest rod holding their pot of snails over the fire.

Then a travelling shaman stole the heart of Sho's wife. Every afternoon for a week she followed him into the hills, a middle-aged woman excited and ashamed.

'Perhaps I deserve this,' thought Sho. But the settlement, although new, proved traditional: the adulterers were tied together on the slope, embracing for days until Sho wept and forgave her. The shaman, though, was marched to a pothole choked with bushes, his body crashing out of sight through thorn and bracken and splashing into unseen water.

Later the woman was forced into the latrine for the unauthorized birth. The shaman had given her a son. She was sent back to her tribe with the child, who she called Jivu Lanu, a Yi name to which he was not entitled.

Sho had said that his wife couldn't produce a boy because she had no hair below, but now it was clear where the problem lay. This shame seemed to break the men of the village. The youngest put on his coloured feathers and gave a long speech against farming, that trade for the careful, and vanished upstream with his family. The others worked all day on the slope then sat without words in the leaking huts.

There were few pregnancies and the children always died. Every funeral brought arguments: the stream was too rocky to carry away the dead, even a dead baby, so the two wives demanded the rites of their tribe, which involved much firewood and a pollution of the gods of the air.

Then the women grew silent. One returned to her tribe and the last hung herself from a doorpost, having listened to the lonely dead who whisper to the despairing from the world of ghosts.

When he wasn't working, Sho tried to sleep, lying crooked around the leaks from his roof. In the gloomy valley the change of seasons was obscure, and the men lost track of time, toiling stupefied during uncharted years, speechless, eating in the fields like beasts.

One day he stood by the stream. He looked up at their collapsing huts and saw that the seeping hill might feed three men but not four. He pictured a house high on the slope, its people busy and fat, the man with the limp accepted like an uncle.

He walked downstream for an hour then slept under a bush. He walked all night, slipping on wet stones at the river's edge, and came to the midstream rock where he had fished long ago with an incense stick for a timer.

He stayed for a year, dozing all day then fishing in the dark with tricks from his boyhood – catching crayfish with bits of crayfish, or weaving traps from reeds and a twig, or trailing his fingers under a bank until they were cold as weeds and the fish slid among them to sleep. He ate his catches raw because he dared not light a fire, but was seen by the local tribe and moved his camp to a side valley downstream, moving twice more, wasting years because he was ashamed to meet his father.

But his father was dead and the village full of women. They accepted Sho because he could handle a boat and lead the ceremonies for the ancestors, though he was odd and old-seeming and for weeks slept in the bushes as he had during his years alone. One of the women was his uncle's youngest daughter and had a well-made hut. He was afraid of her because she was pretty and mad, but one hot night he crept to her bed: she was half asleep and called him 'father'.

The four older women had taken the best boats and the easiest fishing grounds. He had to use his father's stupid boat, the only spare, and to struggle in the swift waters off the far bank. His hands, soft as mushrooms in the perpetual damp upriver, grew dry and hard. His skin tightened in the sunshine and his clothes lost the smell of mould. The oars fitted like a handshake. In the third year he had a child, though only a daughter.

But the four aunts were a trial. They had emerged from their struggles with the river and lay in their boats in the sunshine, pressing a fishing line against the planks with their bare feet, pressing tight enough to feel a fish yet not too tight to drop the line if it snagged on driftwood. Only men should use boats, but the aunts used one hand to scull while the other aimed a spear or – with a casual flick – sent a net spinning over the water, all its hem cutting the surface at once, so that the fish fled inwards and were trapped. They shouted their gossip across the water, though not to him, and watched as his net landed askew and fish escaped from its lopsided splash.

They had married into the fisher folk from a migrant tribe which had camped on the ridge above the beach, clearing the brush for crops and leaving when the thin soil washed away. This tribe came from the hills, so their fish goddess was a minor deity, only notable because she was married to the river god and caused him much annoyance. The fisher folk believed that fish were the sons of a male god, but the aunts told their new husbands that fish were created when the goddess was stepping over the river and saw her reflection.

Their husbands, obliged to go on the dangerous water, hated these jokes so the aunts kept silent, though they teased their men by blaming the goddess for every misfortune. When their husbands died they were ashamed, but had lately begun to mention the goddess again, angering Sho, who remembered his youth when it was unquestioned that everything that lived had crawled from the river: only the fish god had stayed at home, being the river's favourite son.

In revenge he pretended that he couldn't tell the women apart. They had their distinctions – who laughed if he saw them making water from the boat, who liked fish eyes, and who had first welcomed Jivu Lanu. And they argued, so that the two fishing partnerships split and re-formed, and sometimes one of the women stamped around the beach while her partner struggled on the river: he watched these squabbles with satisfaction. But the women came from the same tribe, had been weathered by the same wind and sun, had a notched front tooth from tying line, and were square as sacks in their hempen jackets and wide hempen trousers – so he called them 'you old aunts'.

The women were surprised but then adopted the name, saying, 'Yes, we are like sisters,' and calling his wife 'Little Niece'.

Baffled again, Sho brooded about women and fishing,

and how women shouldn't touch boats, still less sit in them, least of all during their monthly flow. As he fished he addressed the dead menfolk of the village, sharing their indignation because their widows used the boats every day of the month and stored them under the houses without precautions.

'If a woman is in a house, then a boat shouldn't go under it,' murmured Sho to his dead listeners. 'But of course we know that thieves are clever and watchdogs eat a lot of fish. This is why you stored the boats under the houses but took precautions.' The forefathers would remember how they stood the boats on their sterns, leaning slightly forwards, so that the bow and keel deflected the down-flowing pollution from the women, which ran into the beach and thence to the river, to be carried to the dirty places downstream. Older men, being less strong, had merely turned their boats upside down with a leafy branch forked over them, reasoning that their wives were also old and drying up.

But none of the men would go under their houses while a woman was inside, except for some very weak men who wore hats made of leafy twigs and were ashamed. Yet even the weakest man would not allow a woman into his boat: the dead menfolk must agree that their boats should now be burned, though this was not really possible and instead a ceremony lasting many days would have to suffice, involving a fire of herbs and odorous wood under the upturned boats.

And Sho told the forefathers how the aunts even sabotaged his own precautions. He was too self-conscious to stand his boat on its stern: it was anyway ridiculously heavy. But surely it was not unreasonable to turn the boat upside down. Yet often in the mornings he would find the boat right-way up, and the aunts smirking. Then he would have to ask his wife if her blood was flowing.

From the first, the aunts had called him 'headman', though he was never confident they would obey him, only that they would pretend to. But it was shameful to be the only man amongst females, and worse to be their leader, absurd as herding chickens. And the village was blighted, because the aunts were mad from lack of men. They hauled big fish ashore saying, 'Welcome, my husband,' and if they found a certain size of fingerling they held it up and said, 'You must come home with me, still twisting.'

But Sho was afraid of the river. His father had said that every generation a man was drowned, becoming a recruit for the river god or a recompense to the fish god who lost so many soldiers to the fisher folk. But no men had been drowned for years, because they were all dead. Their bodies had been given to the river, so perhaps the river god or fish god was satisfied, but perhaps the gods were still hungry.

And the river here was wide and purposeful. It was deep as a man is tall, so that a man would drown on tiptoe, dancing downstream until the river narrowed and deepened beyond the bend and he was danced off his feet as if hanged. If he fell in during the winter drought, or nearer the shore, then he might crouch against the current for a moment, his wake like a cloak, until he was dragged off and beaten against rocks. But usually he would vanish so quickly that even his fishing partner wouldn't see – or might pretend not to see, because a man's oars should be thrown in after him.

His father and uncle had discussed this endlessly. Oars, after all, are hard to make. And wasn't it always too late to throw them in? And could a boat return to shore with no oars? Yet what if the man survived, even without his oars to hold, and came home and found the oars still aboard, especially if he shared the boat with his own brother?

So the headman hated to fish, and was glad when the white man went on the river alone, leaving the catch for Sho and his family – though this was at the same time irritating, because it showed how the foreigner was rich and childish and thought that fishing was a game.

While the white ghost was fishing, Sho fussed around the beach, and once swilled away some of the fish offal, remembering the old headman's lapse into irrelevance. He spoke impatiently to that idler Jivu Lanu, who was servicing the aunts, each in turn or all together. He muttered a comparison between the aunts' boats and their slack old bodies, and thereafter ignored the so-called shaman, who couldn't answer the most worrying of all theological questions – whether they lived on the main river or a tributary.

But now he hated the river. He recalled a saying of his childhood, and murmured, 'The river is the father but the mountains are the mother.' He stood on the beach and looked at the hills that had cradled his childhood.

The river, though, was a permanent stranger that he was sick of fighting.

So he cleared the overgrown vegetable patch on the slope above the beach, pretending an indignation: 'Fishing is easy,' he told Little Niece, gesturing at the aunts on the river, 'but someone must grow the vegetables.' One day he dumped a load of bamboo on the edge of the beach, cut from a grove on a hillside upstream, throwing it down as if angry. Then he remembered his father, so that the logs grew brown and became a home for rats.

In fact the aunts had decided that they would no longer cut bamboo or raise vegetables or lay out fish traps and night lines and staked nets. With most of the village dead there was plenty of fish, which they sold at Market Village, spending their earnings at once unless headman Sho was there. They bought clothes instead of cloth, meat instead of traps, tools instead of iron, vegetables instead of seed, and thereby impressed the tribals, who sat at Market Village for days, waiting for the riverboat whose schedule they could never understand and for the market which was timed for its coming.

The headman resented the wealth of the aunts, which seemed another reason why women shouldn't fish and was somehow connected to his young wife, whose desires were relentless and unnecessary.

And today she had ridden with the white giant. He told himself that he didn't really mind: it was just that his boat was now polluted like the rest.

11

Grace hated Chinese food, so Yue Fat's dinner party was an ordeal. Secretary Chang, with many sidelong smirks to his master, cleared a space at the table to demonstrate her game with the character for happiness. She was invited to explain its significance.

Afterwards she wrote: *I ignored the invitation of Chang, whom it is hard not to dislike, instead explaining that I had discovered similar provocative examples, and, taking the brush and paper from the little secretary (with no superfluous courtesy!), I showed how the ancient character for ship,* 船, *comprises the character for boat,* 舟, *alongside that for the number eight,* 八, *and that for mouth,* 口. *In short, the archetypal Chinese ship contains eight mouths or eight people.*

I then briefly told the story of Noah's Ark, and counted those saved from the Flood by God's mercy: Noah and his wife; their sons, Ham, Shem and Japheth; and their three wives. Eight, of course.

At this, Yue Fat laughed heartily and clapped his hands. Grace was further disconcerted because the youngest of Yue Fat's three soldiers now brought a cherry-wood box. Chuckling, Yue undid its ivory clasps and lifted out a grey silk bundle. He loosened cotton ribbons to show a scroll of mulberry paper, soft and spongy with age, wrapped around two black-wood rods. With a smile of pleasure he began to unroll it.

At first they saw only isolated triangles of black ink, some with tiny figures in conical hats: 'These are ships on the sea,' said Yue, though John frowned in bewilderment. Then two whiskered lines appeared, closing together as Yue Fat unwound the scroll. 'Do you understand?' he said. 'It is the mouth of the river.'

Grace declined to be silent: *I pointed out that, as well as the word for happiness, many other characters contain 'garden' as an element – including devil,* 鬼, *fruit,* 果, *naked,* 裸, *and tempter,* 魔.

The readers of this journal will need no prompting to be reminded of that primal tragedy, the Fall of Man, whose dismal story I then outlined to my dining companions. 'Such occurrences are beyond coincidence,' I declared.

Suddenly John understood the scroll. There were cliffs, a pagoda, ragged islands that he half recognized, and squares that must be houses. 'When this was painted, Hong Kong was small,' said Yue.

'Canton!' said John, and indeed here was his home, a nest of squares among the threads of the delta.

Now the scroll took them upstream, into windings of the river which John had never seen. The grey paper showed islands and tributaries, more junks and fishing boats, the wrinkles of rapids, and towns which Yue named with an indulgent chuckle.

Grace imposed herself again: *I said that the beginning of Man was the most important beginning of all, as was shown by a Chinese character for first, 先, which I sketched on the paper, showing how it comprised the characters for dust, 土, live, 丿, and man, 儿, (this latter being derived from the more familiar 人). I then recited from memory the thrilling lines from Genesis of how 'the Lord God formed man of the dust of the ground'.*

The scroll was now vague. It had taken them far from the coast and civilization, and the river's curves were suspiciously regular. Yue Fat smiled: 'I believe that our little settlement might be here, though there is little to confirm it.' He was pointing to another smooth curve in the river, with – on its outer side – a tiny black triangle depicting a mountain.

I said, 'These demonstrations of the Genesis story in Chinese characters are the product of only a short period of study. I expect to discover more and stronger instances, encouraged by the thought that China's script is the oldest part of its culture, so that its knowledge of Genesis predates everything we now think of as Chinese, including the teachings of the Buddha and Confucius (whom I always call "Confuse us").'

John said, 'In the West, rivers don't change their names along their course, like rivers in China. It's like a Chinese man can have a milk name, then a school name and a marriage name and a name after his death. In the West, men and rivers have only one name.'

Wishing to heighten their enjoyment of the map, I described how, after the Flood, Noah's grandson, Phut, left his family because of a dispute, his descendants spreading east to people the Orient, including China.

Since Cantonese is the oldest of China's languages, it follows that the Children of Israel came first to these Southern provinces, their easiest route being down this very river.

The scroll had reached the mountains. The river unravelled into tributaries, and there were little pine trees, hermits in coloured robes, and caves with monsters winged and fanged. At last the river dwindled to nothing at the watershed, and the paper was blank.

'This white is the snow of the mountains, perhaps,' said Yue with a smile.

'Or it means that there is nothing interesting beyond China,' said John.

Yue laughed, then said, 'But look as we unroll further.'

There was writing: first a red stamp stained the blank snow of the paper. It was the artist's signature, followed by his account of the work: nine weeks were required to paint it, during which he had ridden on nine riverboats, visited nine riverside towns, and consulted nine times nine mandarins, one of whom wore the violet robe and peacock feather. Then came writings from its first owner, a court official, then the next and the next, poem and essay and poem again, interpretations of the painting or expressions of joy at its beauty. John was absorbed, and the scroll trailed from either end of the table and down to Yue's best carpet.

I explained, moreover, that Phut left the Holy Lands before the destruction of the Tower of Babel, and thus escaped the divine punishment suffered by its builders, whose folly caused the Lord to distort and divide the language He had given to Adam, which had been the universal language of mankind. It follows that the languages of China are directly descended from the tongue spoken by God and Adam in the Garden of Eden!

Now the meal began – tiny dishes brought by the soldier-servants and commended to her by secretary Chang. His smile seemed derisive as he named each course, always from strange creatures or strange parts of creatures. And how mocking was Yue Fat, watching her as the food glistened in its dishes, then lay inert in her mouth, its texture like a tongue.

Until now, I said, these ideas have not been welcomed by the Chinese, who prefer to believe that their noble civilization sprang directly from the soil of China. But if there are elements of the Genesis story in Chinese characters, as my discoveries suggest, then no honest man can dismiss the Christian God as a lie of the foreign devils.

The great carp arrived, bought from the fisher women and now appropriately rank, served with its head attached, eyes shrivelled by the oven.

Instead the Chinese will see that in embracing Christianity, they are returning to the God of their ancestors!

They were given live crayfish, which leapt in bowls of vinegar, wine and sesame oil.

Chang composed himself, which always prefigured an essay into English, and said, 'My master would like to know how the lady enjoys her fish.'

At this point Grace hurried from the room.

'You will know of the sage Lu Shang,' said Chang,

turning smoothly to John. 'He fished with a straight hook so that the fish might chose whether to die. Yet such was his virtue that the fish hurried to sacrifice themselves.'

John got up, bowing to the company, and followed his wife. She was outside, a handkerchief at her mouth. She was ill, she said, and must go home. John hesitated, then said he would return to the meal.

In the dining room he explained his wife's indisposition. The conversation had faltered, but wine had made him indifferent. His glass was refilled. Again the secretary was whispering in his ear. How odd that the little man would ignore his master for these private talks.

Perhaps the secretary was also drunk, because he gave John a book, bound in pink silk. John took a moment to understand the pictures. A little drunk and dizzy, he stared stupidly. What were these white, whiskered parts?

It was pornography. Elegant men and women lay among the blocks of text, coupling below their lifted robes. He was glad of his drunkenness, which saved embarrassment. He stood up with a sigh, bowed to the company and walked from the house.

He stood swaying outside. Down the slope he could see his own roof, and off in the dark was the fisher folk village. He thought how, in his own house, he felt a consciousness of the collector, who, being higher, had an advantage: the fisher folk must likewise be aware of the missionaries above. This was the philosophy of Wind and Water, he decided, whose teachings were common sense.

Through the wooden walls he heard a raised voice. It was secretary Chang, lecturing his master.

Chang had been in Yue Fat's service for a year, his ingenuity bent to the great project of a return to civilization. Like Grace and John he had come to the pebble beach expecting a busy town and many responsibilities. Instead justice was administered by village headmen, while sanitation, transport and water supply were managed by the river.

There was nothing to do but wait for the poppies to ripen and the tax to fall due, and he saw how Yue Fat had been so bored that he couldn't recover, like a man who has been too frightened. Chang dreaded this stupor, and bustled to stay awake.

First he guided the collector in the introduction of river licences, which they described as being 'for the discouragement of over-fishing' and which brought a few coins each month from the fisher folk. Then he began enquiries about Market Village, the Yi opium plantation in the next valley.

The Yi had once owned only a few slaves, mostly Miao, who had worked in the poppy fields alongside the Yi and were well treated and allowed their own rites at marriage and death. But they were ungrateful and tried to escape, so at night they were shackled in houses as strong as the master's, and in the daytime were watched by overseers with whips. These expenses could only be recouped in one way: more slaves were acquired and the Yi no longer learnt their names.

The plantation had passed through sons and grandsons, and now there were three Yi families side by side. Sometimes the opium stores were looted by drunken tribesmen, but Imperial troops made punitive raids and the problem eased, though there was always petty theft from the fields.

So the Yi were rich. They owned the only flat ground in a day's walk, and could charge the stallholders at the market, which nevertheless grew. They lent money to local tribes and took children as security: often the youngsters were forfeit and sold into slavery in the Yi homelands, far upriver in the Cool Mountains. Recently they had raised stones from the river and built a storehouse, exacting rent from the boats which took their opium: a fat man sat by the door, smoking his wages and guarding the Imperial packages – preserved delicacies and official mail – which Yue Fat's soldiers came to collect.

Chang had gone with them once, then visited the Yi patriarch, noting his tiled roof, his stone floors, and the silver jewellery on his young wives, who were so numerous that they had their own house, though its roof was thatched. Next day the corporal had returned to the patriarch with notification that a tax was payable on all markets in the Empire: soon a pleasing gift arrived for Yue Fat. The corporal went again, this time with word of a renewed Imperial ban on opium: there was no inordinate protest before the Yi began a monthly subvention, though they started to level their fields for rice. Then Chang thought of the riverport.

With dread the Yi patriarch received another letter from the hands of the corporal, who did not bow. Again it had been written by Chang but signed by Yue Fat, and pointed out that the great river flowed straight and swift past the Yi port, which was therefore most hazardous for the riverboats, which strained on their mooring cables against the rushing current: moreover, the mouth of the Yi valley was flat and low, so that in the winter drought it was full of boulders and in summer it was flooded. As a father guards his children so the Empire guards its people: wooden piles must be driven into the river bed to secure the boats, and quays must be built out of bamboo baskets full of stones.

This matter brought the eldest sons of the patriarch to Yue Fat: they carried gifts and drank much tea. Discussions were held concerning an Emperor's mandate from heaven and how it was devolved to the most distant official. Yue Fat enjoyed these discussions, which reminded him of his schooldays, though the Yi were amusingly incapable and were grateful when secretary Chang suggested an insurance scheme. Instead of the crushing expense of the bamboo baskets and wooden piles, a surety was paid by the Yi and held by the collector.

Chang reported these exactions to his superiors in Canton. He would therefore have to remit to them a part of his invented taxes, but was desperate to show his loyalty and cunning, and to be moved from this backwater. In turn he was contemptuous of Yue Fat, who showed no aptitude for promotion.

In particular he grew suspicious of Yue's record in the Imperial examinations: the examiners of Canton were notoriously open to bribery, which they described as 'book gold' or 'conveyancing expenses' or 'small expenses for opening the door'. Chang saw that his petulance grew from this dismal isolation at the beach, but couldn't help himself.

He brooded most about his own struggles. His father had been a poor shopkeeper, to whom Chang's long fingers had seemed an omen of brilliance. While the child still bore his milk-name of Dog, chosen to confuse devils, he had been given the Four Treasures of the Study – paper, brush, ink, and ink stone – and an itinerant scholar was paid to write giant characters on the walls around his crib. As he grew he was told of the student ploughman who had tied his book between the horns of his buffalo, and of the peasant who – having studied by the light of a glow-worm and kept himself awake by tying his hair to a roof beam – had risen to the highest office.

At fourteen he travelled to the Imperial examinations in Canton. He was stripped and his hair was combed for hidden cribs: the seams of his clothes were cut open. He turned his face to the wall and recited from the Five Classics, the Thirteen Classics and the Three-Characters Classics.

He was sealed in a cell two paces long by one wide which stood in a walled field of 8,652 identical cells, each with a student and his store of rice, tea, candles, cakes, lamp oil and bedding. Chang stayed for thirty-six hours, sleeping on the plank which served as his desk. His first essay subjects were: 'He who is sincere is intelligent, and the intelligent will be faithful'; and 'A man from his youth studies eight principles. When he arrives at manhood he wishes to reduce them to practice'; and 'The sound of the oar and the green of the hills and water'.

Like Yue, Chang succeeded. For seven years he rose through the Imperial hierarchy, finally serving in Hong Kong as an intermediary between the Imperial administration and the British – a far more prestigious post than his present master's.

But he had been taught nothing of geography, mathematics, science and foreign languages. He read *Scientific American* and the Macmillan science books, and he noted how a wilful blindness was maintained even by the mandarins of the Treaty Ports, who saw the barbarians daily. Thus, over tea at his elegant family home outside Canton, Yue Fat declared that European uniforms were so tight that soldiers who fell over couldn't get up. His father's influential friends replied with another familiar dictum: the whites could always be brought to heel because, addicted to dairy foods, they would die of constipation without Chinese tea and rhubarb.

'Perhaps my son is not the most energetic of boys,' said Yue Fat's father, alone with his friends. 'Therefore my family would be grateful for any post, even in the interior.'

Meanwhile Chang had declared once too often that ignorance crippled China in its struggle against the foreigners. His superiors, growing indignant, sent him to this wilderness.

Later they remembered his facility with the barbarians. A letter arrived at the pebble beach: it was from Canton, and was greeted by Yue Fat with incense and the striking of a little bell, since the written word is equal in honour to the man who sends it. Among more important matters it had instructions for secretary Chang: he had been chosen to supervise two missionaries, whose work he must impede.

12

'Some die bearing sons or daughters, some die with blood-soaked clothing, some die with blood-soaked groins.' Jivu was speaking in his tribal language, so that no one understood the exorcism except his father's ghost. To the fisher folk, though, the ceremony seemed all the more impressive.

'Some die crushed by trees or stones, some die of thirst or hunger, some swell and burst, some hang and burst, some are stabbed or slashed, some trip and crush their heads, some die of loud shouts or big words, some are roasted by fire, some are swept away by floods.

'Tile-roofed houses burn, thatch-roofed houses burn. At work on the road they step on mating snakes. At work on the mountain they are crushed by falling trees. Some have intestines ruptured by poison.'

Jivu Lanu and the aunts had crowded into the headman's house. Jivu Lanu was pointing a thorn bush at Little Niece, who crouched in a corner. She looked beautiful and frightened, and this was exciting. 'Pain floods her head, her body and feet. An entire family harmed. The harm centres on her bed. She can't sleep, can't sit a moment, can't stretch her legs, can't lift her hands. Her food won't digest, her drink won't stay down, her bones have no marrow.

'The pain has been seen in the pulse of the left wrist and the lines of the left hand, in the cock's beak and goat's shoulder blade, in grain and in rice, in a chunk of salt, a bowl of wine, a pot of wine, a stick of incense, squatting on the table's corner and crouching on a pack-saddle.'

Jivu drew himself up for the great accusation, at last confronting his father. 'You white-haired stud ghost, yellow-fanged bitch ghost, scruffy-thighed bitch ghost! Ghost of nine mares, of seven cats, of seven dogs, biting, clawing, entangling, maddening – it is you!'

Now he knelt and whispered. He was telling his father's ghost about the gifts he had brought – all imaginary. 'Offerings of magpies, pheasants, fish, shrimp, wild geese and ducks, jays, crows, green pigeons, frogs, bull-frogs, bees, ants, grasshoppers, long-tailed dragonflies, a flapping hen and struggling cock, three hundred pine branches as long as an arm, twelve sticks marked with faces, twelve marked with ears, twelve marked with dog's claws and tiger claws, three hundred white bowls of tea and three hundred white bowls of the best alcohol bought from Chinese merchants.

'The sky's seven corners, the earth's four sides, take my offerings back to the sky, take my offerings back to the earth.'

He swept the room with the thorned branches, declaring, 'I drive you from the roof peak: descend from the roof peak. I drive you from the beam's corners. I drive you from the walls. I sweep you with pine branches, thrust thorns in your eyes, snare your neck with dog-shit vines.'

He kicked open the little straw door: 'I drive you over the threshold. The yard's head, the yard's tail, I drive you. That corner, that side, I drive you. This end, this side, don't stay there! That end, that side, don't stand there!'

He stepped into the doorway and waved his thorns to drive the ghost down the ladder. He began the most important part of the ceremony, which reminded the ghost that the river was its rightful road. 'Come out through the gate, out along eleven gullies, out through twelve streams. Descend to the ridges, descend to the long roads. I drive you, ghost, drive you to the river.'

And the river was full of the welcoming corpses of animals. 'Your companions live there, your ancestors live there. Return to those sandy beaches. Three pairs of dogs die there, three pairs of boars and wildcats die. Three pairs of rabbits and weasels die, three pairs of mares die, three pairs of cats die.

'Three bubbling streams merge, twelve great rivers merge. Shrimp play in three places: your ghost friends are there. White fish play in three places: your ghost companions are there. Little officials in the river centre, friends of officials in the river centre. They wear silk clothing. They hold red flags. They wave green flags.

'Follow the river, you ghost. We give you the river as your steed. Ride the river like a fine white horse.'

Now he pointed downstream with the thorn bush. He listed the attractions of the rich cities along the river. 'Wuxuan holds a market on the day of the dog. Nine days of revelry, nine days of drinking. Drinking the finest tea, drunk on the day of the snake. Little ghosts in the street, ghost officials in the street: in one day they kill three goats. More meat than they can eat, piled like sand on a beach. They await your coming, ghost. They will wait until the ghost comes.

'Pingnan holds a market on the day of the mouse. They bring out *dans* of rice for you, bring out *dous* of buckwheat, bring out *shengs* of grain, offer bowls of salt. Stretch out your apron: don't loose it through holes in the cloth. Stretch out your hands: don't loose it between your fingers. Walk about and sell it. Ghost shirts over there. Ghost hats over there. Buy ghost shirts to wear. Change your clothing. Change your overcoats.'

Now came the names of towns that none of them had seen, semi-legendary places, far downstream, full of dazzling wealth, leading the ghost on to ever richer cities, luring it to the sea, which was its dissolution. 'Go down to Wuzhou. Your ghost officials are there. Embroidery needles and thread, every kind of earring, bracelets and rings, shoes of every style. More clothing than you can wear, piles of silk, looms and spindles.

'Go down to Canton. Your ghost king lives there. Every day they hold meetings in Canton. Your king is over there.

'I shall lead you down to Hong Kong. Go to where your ghost companions live. If the road returns, don't you return. If the road strays, don't you stray.'

Jivu Lanu led the aunts down from the headman's house. He had put a circle of ashes around the bottom of the ladder: this would warn away visitors and also show the passage of ghosts. The ashes weren't disturbed, but of course ghosts are cunning, none more so than the ghost of a shaman.

He had shown his father the pleasures of the river, and now listed the inadequacies of the beach. He pointed with the thorn bush and said, 'Look over at that slope, only cliffs and caves. Look at this slope, only thorns and brambles. No land to turn a plough, rocks below the feet, cliffs at every corner.'

He pointed back up the ladder to the headman's house. 'Look at the bed's head: the bed's head stinks. Look at the bed's tail: the bed's tail has vomit. Her hair reeks of sweat, her feet stink of rot. She eats goat meat, drinks horse soup, lies on goatskins, stuffs her pillow with pepper, burns pepper branches for firewood, boils pepper leaves for soup. An evil place to live, you white-haired stud ghost, you yellow-fanged bitch ghost.'

Jivu began to improvise in his bad Cantonese. 'Little Niece is mad. Her womb is no home for you. She talks to the river. She takes the Jesus medicine, so that her ancestors are alone and cold! What daughter lets her ancestors go hungry?'

Little Niece and headman Sho sat in their house. Sho leapt up and closed their door, but in a straw house you can hear everything.

'Little Niece is mad,' said Jivu Lanu. 'Leave her. Her family is dead but she forgets them. She forgets her daughter. Leave her rotten womb.'

Little Niece felt that she had gone somewhere where the words couldn't hurt. Water roared in her ears and her face was smoothed away like the face of her dead father. She had come to her still spot in the river, and only noticed that the aunts were laughing.

'She goes fishing with the white giant!' Jivu shouted. 'She likes his big back. O spirit, you must leave her womb before a big white horse comes prodding you!'

Grace and John had come to the beach but found it deserted. They had heard talking inside the headman's hut, and then saw the procession down the ladder. Perhaps it was some communal celebration: an anniversary perhaps, or a blessing for the headman's house. Grace said, 'These rituals can often be adapted to Christianity.'

Then Jivu Lanu spoke in Cantonese and they understood the ceremony. Grace thought how Jesus had expelled evil spirits, and how this exorcism might help Little Niece, who was unhappy. Then she heard Jivu's final triumphant shout.

13

Next morning a letter came from Canton. John had watched from the headman's boat as two Miao slaves appeared on the track from Market Village and struggled up the slope to the collector's house, no doubt with the usual sacks of coal and boxes of tea, salt, sugar and tobacco.

Coming home an hour later, he found the letter on the path outside the Mission House, weighted by a stone and presumably left by one of the soldiers. He pushed the letter among the scraps of fishing kit in his jacket pocket, and instead read the Boxer pamphlet which had been put with it as an insult.

It showed a man being beheaded while he clutched a cross. Below, in jagged letters, it declared, 'The iron roads and iron carriages are disturbing the terrestrial dragon and the earth's beneficial influences. The rust which drips from telegraph wires is the blood of the outraged spirits of the air. Missionaries steal the eyes, marrow and heart to make medicines. Whoever drinks a glass of tea at the parsonage is struck by death: the brains burst out of the skull.'

John pushed the leaflet into his pocket: he would not show it to Grace. He was sitting with a dish of tea in their kitchen when he remembered the letter, still in his jacket, which he always left on the veranda because Grace said it smelled of fish.

The envelope was stained with coal dust from the soldier's thumb. She wrinkled her nose and said, 'It's from your wonderful Mr Burkett.'

She read aloud: '*Dear brother and sister, I trust that your holy work is proceeding with the success which your brothers and sisters here have all predicted for you.*

'*But I have a sad duty to perform, one that will touch most immediately on the bold young John. Your beloved "amah", Song Lan, has passed to her reward.*'

'Oh, my poor John,' said Grace.

She continued: '*You will be sad, but will be comforted that, late in life, she was brought to a knowledge of the one true God, who alone brings eternal peace, and that she now lays safe on Abraham's bosom after the rocks and shoals of life's voyage. She may not meet many compatriots in the afterlife, but – with your help – the ever-swelling numbers of Chinese converts will join her in times to come. Be brave, dear John: one day ye shall be reunited with your beloved foster parent.*'

His first reaction was anger. Burkett's petty voice, his lisping dentures, drove him down the slope to the beach and then, under the bewildered eyes of the fisher folk, over the headland to the place where they drew their water. He paced there, hands covering his ears, until Grace appeared with a stricken face on the headland, mouthing in silence like a puppet.

He blundered upstream for an hour. A rapid roared

like an avalanche, and he sat close so that its thunder filled his head.

Jivu Lanu was content after the exorcism. He was ready to start back upriver, so at dusk he sat with the aunts around their driftwood fire and shared his last insights.

First he flattered them, saying that their village was cupped in the perfect armchair shape of hills – behind it was the Hog and to its left the headland. It was true, he said, that on the right there was no sheltering hill, only the uneven levels of the bank, but it was always good if the tiger land on the right was lower than dragon land on the left, and was therefore subdued. And, he agreed, some might also find fault with the mountain on the far bank, as being rather high: but it was good to be sheltered from the *qi* of passing spirits, which were especially strong in a mountain region, especially the north dragon, a creature he had never liked.

In any case, he said, everything was compensated by the river. Hearing this the aunts leant forward. Jivu Lanu moved his arm to show how the river came and departed through mountains, as recommended by the wisest geomancers, and thereby conveyed the *qi* into and through the village, and how it formed the perfect curve in front of them, conforming to the philosophy of Wind and Water which declared that water should be like a jade belt around a settlement and would thus bring good fortune for five generations. A little of its water meanwhile passed through the bodies of people and animals, where its *qi* turned their organs like waterwheels.

Only mountain people, such as himself and the fisher folk, could harness the *qi* of the upland river, which made powerful fish that passed their vigour to those who ate them. It was essential, though, that the fisher folk retain their strength, so that they could tame the *qi* and not be broken by it. And here he cautioned them about the two missionaries, who couldn't flourish so far upstream, where the earth dragon was close to the surface and its *qi* was strong, throwing up mountains and making earthquakes and requiring to be tamed by medicine which the God-believers didn't know.

The whites, he said, would cause disturbances to the flow, being creatures of straight lines – railway tracks and telegraph wires and mineshafts, and the iron crosses on their churches that made a path for the devils of the air. And the whites were plotting to straighten the river, he said: its *qi* would then flow to their towns on the coast, and their warships could come even here, to this beach. The aunts were sceptical but nevertheless wondered if their headman, who was such a friend to the white giant, was able to lead them.

As they talked, little Shen sat happily among them. But Jivu pointed to the child and said, 'She will soon die.'

He explained that Shen had been damaged by the wicked ghost which had lived in her mother's womb until driven out by his most skilful exorcism. When the child died she must be buried under a path, so that passing feet would disperse the bad *qi*; or she might be put in a tree to be taken by crows and ravens; or, best of all, she could be chopped into pieces and scattered. The aunts laughed, disbelieving him, but said that her body could be thrown in the river: they would use the river downstream from the village, so that her bad *qi* would be carried away.

They noticed Little Niece looking down from her house. They hadn't seen her since the exorcism, and she seemed more mad. She must have heard their words because she shouted, 'The white people saved my daughter.'

'She cannot live long,' answered Jivu Lanu.

'You are wrong,' said Little Niece. Her madness made her beautiful, and for once the aunts listened. 'You are wrong because my daughter is well.'

'You must go back to Canton,' said Grace.

'I was very stupid,' said John. 'Very wrong.'

'You must go back to Canton. I will stay here and continue our mission.'

'Surely this is unnecessary.'

'You cannot preach to these people. They won't believe you, having seen your actions.'

She was crying, and felt sick as she cried. She had been carrying water from the river when Little Niece, so sly and deceitful, had waved to her. She had drawn Grace across the beach, and up the ladder to the headman's house, and had thrown open the door. John was kneeling on the cane floor. He was kneeling and whispering in front of the grubby little altar, and might have been praying in a Christian church except that ribbons were round his neck and on the altar was the fish god. Grace had turned home without a word, refusing to reveal anything to these people. But now came the reckoning.

She said, ' "Thou shalt worship the Lord thy God, and Him only shalt thou serve." '

'It was a stupid little thing,' said John.

' "He that toucheth pitch shall be defiled therewith." '

'I didn't speak. I was silent. I said nothing.'

'But you don't see that toleration is no virtue,' she said. 'I'm ashamed. I will go into the mountains. I will work among the poor people in the mountains.'

She looked at him through her tears, and shuddered at what she had seen: the dirty altar; the dumb god of the fishes. 'The Israelites travelled among heathens. The Lord said, "If thou forget the Lord thy God, and walk after other gods, ye shall surely perish." '

'I was stupid. It was because of my loss. I will fight ignorance and superstition.'

But he repented only because he had hurt her. She said, 'Leave me. I can't look at you.'

After a while she took up her journal, but didn't mention this horror. She wrote: *We say 'in vino veritas', meaning that an inebriated man tells the truth. I am no Latin scholar, but might one not say 'in extremis veritas', meaning that at some pitch of emotion – grief, perhaps, or fear or anger – a man will turn to the god he most values? However, these things are perhaps difficult to put into words.*

How curious that 'angered' is an anagram of 'enraged'!

Then she turned to earlier pages, trembling as she read of the days of her happiness.

14

At dawn the next day, John was back on the beach. He had been awake all night. In the darkness Grace had laid a hand on his shoulder, but he didn't move and at last she fell asleep. At first light he had come to stare over the grey water and think about his amah and his life and how cowardice had bought him here. He heard the huts creaking as the fisher folk stirred, but didn't want to talk and dragged out the headman's boat.

Suddenly Little Niece leapt aboard. 'Go,' she whispered.

He had no strength to argue. And she was so pretty. He pushed the boat into the water, then took his place amidships, rowing them to the great mooring rock near the far bank as the woman crouched low among the dirty gear. He dropped the oars and snared the pole with the prow rope, then turned to the woman. But she ignored him, sitting amidships, her face turned away.

He moved to the stern to sort his fishing lines. He was baiting hooks and checking floats when he saw that the oars were missing.

Puzzled, he went amidships to look more closely. Each oar should have been held between a pair of vertical wooden bars at the gunwales. Bamboo rope was wound in figures of eight between the bars, and the oars inserted below them. Yet the ropes and oars had gone.

He looked downstream, but the oars would be far away. He turned to the woman, who had moved to the prow, wanting to question her or to say that there was no danger, that the fisher folk would bring them fresh oars. But she was turned away, hunched over, her shoulders working.

'No,' he shouted. 'Stop.'

But the boat had ceased its battle with the river. Little Niece had cut the mooring rope, and they were racing downstream.

Grace was asleep when headman Sho burst in. She was dragged to the floor and shouted at. She called for John, but received only the headman's laughter.

'Your husband has gone with my wife,' he said, and laughed through his tears. 'Your husband is tupping my wife, tupping her now.' He sat on her floor and wept.

Grace pulled a skirt over her nightshift and went to the veranda: she couldn't see her husband. From inside the headman shouted, 'You are not pretty. Why did you marry a handsome man?'

Striding confidently, refusing to think, she went down to the beach: the headman's boat had gone. The aunts were building a drying rack, the first of the season. Grace called, 'Where is my husband?' But they looked in silence.

Grace stared bewildered at the river. She touched her lip, which was bleeding. Her shift was torn. She climbed back up the slope, keeping clear of her house and continuing to the home of Yue Fat. She rapped on his door and the little secretary appeared. She explained the headman's attack, and his strange story about John. Chang's smooth forehead wrinkled. He said regretfully that he knew nothing.

He watched as she went back down the slope, his hands in his sleeves, his frown like a knot in a lady's handkerchief. He was a little disappointed: for all his schemes, the barbarians had been undone by their own gross appetite. He would not intervene, so that the fugitives might copulate.

Again skirting her house, Grace went down to the river. She wanted to ask the aunts about John, but stopped at the edge of the beach because the headman was sitting under his house looking insane.

It was the first hot day. The pebbles were white with the winter drought, but summer rain swept briefly over the valley. Big drops glittered in the sun, so that the aunts shrieked as they laid fish on the drying rack. The gutted fish were like the books she had aired in Hong Kong, but lay under a fur of flies, which – also like fur – stirred in the wind.

The aunts looked at her and laughed.

'Little Niece, help,' said John.

They were speeding downstream. John steered with a fishing scoop, but it was useless. Bounced and jostled, blinded by spray, they spun among midstream rocks.

'Little Niece, we will sink.' But she lay along the flat planks and stared at him.

Headlands reached for them and were flung away, tiny beaches vanished before he could act. The boat drifted side-on as cold water slapped his face and slid over the gunwales.

There was nowhere to land. The river rushed between walls of bare rock that were tall as a man, scoured clean in the floods and only interrupted by colossal boulders and unpredictable inlets of black sand. He stared into the inlets as they flashed past, narrow as caves.

He pulled the scoop from the water and wove bits of rope to its blade, scrabbling in the jumble in the bottom of the boat. Now the scoop had purchase in the water, though its bamboo handle flexed and creaked.

The boat, too slow and square to drive at the shore, floundered heavy-hipped. Yet its thick planks shouldered away boulders and burst the waves like pillows. Water swilled end to end through the tackle amidships and splashed around the woman, who did not move. Without her he could have swum for the bank.

They passed a line of coolies. They were hauling a riverboat up a rapid, scrambling through the shallows with a prow rope over their shoulders. They watched John and the woman with open mouths, but he expected no help: no one would stand between the river god and his prey.

Waves thumped like boxing gloves, but at least it was spring: meltwater from the mountains was deepening the river, so they were cushioned on its fat waters. John's boat tipped down the horrible rapid, but the bulging river made pads around the rocks and shoved them into calmer water.

So they survived. He pushed the tackle over the side,

and now their flat keel skimmed the surface, bumping like a sledge.

They entered a great gorge, the air suddenly cooler, black battlements of stone falling to the water. The river was swifter in its narrow bed, and muttered between the sheer cliffs, almost too low to hear, as the current hurried them along.

At first they seemed safer. Being narrow the river was deep, so that there were no midstream rocks. No headlands projected from the smooth walls of the gorge, and John crouched to bail the water which splashed ankle-deep in the bottom of the boat. He soon regretted this.

The gorge gently bent, and the river, swung outward by the curve, had undercut the cliff, just as it had at the bend at the pebble beach. But here the rock was hard: instead of a scree slope crumbling into the river, it had stayed intact, leaving a prodigious overhang along the waterline.

The boat was also swung outwards. John looked up from his bailing and found the sheer cliffs approaching. He grabbed the scoop, but trees on the cliff face were soon passing above. He could see into the overhang, where eddies, dragged backwards by the rock, were like a river that ran upstream.

He worked frantically with the scoop, but the eddies drew them in. At its outside edge, the ceiling of the overhang was eight or ten feet above the water: the boat was already inside before the scoop could reach it. They were carried further in, bare rock racing past like the tunnels on the railway into China. He glanced deeper into the overhang: in the gloom the ceiling vanished beneath the water.

Now John could push at the ceiling with his hands, which were at once torn. He was driven to his knees, then to his back, kicking against the descending rock. They swept through hanging bats, which flapped at his face and vanished. The boat began to spin. At any moment it would jam and sink.

Suddenly he was blinded by light. Even the woman gave a cry of hope, and John leapt to his feet and looked around. The ceiling had reared up and vanished because here a little stream joined the river.

There was a patch of shingle. He beached them with a final push from his scoop, then leapt ashore and pulled the boat up the shingle. He leant against the prow, his tiredness weighing like wet clothes.

They were at the bottom of a vertical cleft. Somewhere above them, glittering among a tangled jungle, the stream spattered down the cliff face, so fretted by repeated buffets that it filled the cleft with a warm drizzle. Around the patch of beach, dripping ferns arched over fallen boulders, which were clothed in cushions of lush moss. Downstream the dreadful overhang resumed.

The woman was struggling to her feet. He dragged the boat further up the shingle, then helped her out. She stared into his face, her hand on his shoulder as light as a child's. He left her and leant against the rock wall of the inlet, dazed from their escape.

But there was no shelter from the falling water, so he couldn't rest. He took off his jacket and laid it across the blade of the fishing scoop, sewing it in place with fishing line and a straightened hook. He shivered in the mist while Little Niece sat by the boat and watched.

'I'm ready,' she said.

John was dizzied by the river, and saw its lacy siftings, its chuckles and roars, and all this was mixed with his ache for the woman.

At last he said, 'We will go back to the village. Your husband . . .'

'We will go downstream. You and me.' Her boldness brought another slumping of resistance, like another victory of water against the land.

'It's true that we can make no headway upstream against this current,' he murmured. 'And we can't climb the cliffs. So, yes, we have to go on.'

Little Niece sat on the gritty beach, her back very straight. The beach was like a little stage, lit from above, and she seemed to know this, and stared at him without fear, her hair flattened by the falling water. He turned from her gaze and laid his head against the dripping rock, blinking against images of the river, the knots that tightened and relaxed, the lithe reflux and sudden leaps.

But the drizzle pestered him. He roused himself and went to the boat. He checked its planks, then turned it round on the shingle. He tested his scoop in the river as Little Niece climbed aboard, so prompt and bold that again he was helpless.

First they had to escape the overhang which waited downstream of the cleft. John rocked the boat, hefting its weight, and slid it into the water until he felt the tug of the current. He crouched behind the stern, gathering his strength.

He launched the boat, dashing behind it into the shallows. He leapt in and stood amidships, paddling only on the downstream side, aiming towards the upstream edge of the cleft, giving them more room to reach the open river. It was like the way he launched from behind the bend at the pebble beach.

The scoop bit into the river, and they emerged well clear of the overhang. They were swept up by the familiar current, but every stroke of the oar took them further into midstream, and this time he could steer.

They were passing out of the gorge, and the boat tipped down a rapid like a little step. Exhilaration gripped him. In the relief of their escape he forgot his dead amah, his wife, and his desire for the mad woman beside him.

15

They had discussed the matter all morning, Chang enthused, Yue Fat in a familiar state of boredom and worry. Grace had gone back to her house with a soldier as a bodyguard, and Yue's instinct was to ignore it all. But Chang was like a yapping dog.

'The white woman can now be dealt with,' he said vigorously. 'This is a stroke of luck. We must use it.'

Yue said, 'You don't believe her stupid game with the characters.'

'It might destroy the Empire.'

'Her mistakes and misreadings and illiteracy can't . . .'

'Have you forgotten the Taiping Rising, which killed twenty million of the Emperor's subjects?'

'The Taiping!' said Yue Fat derisively, but was ignored.

Chang paced the room, sometimes halting to stare at the river or calling to the young soldier for more tea. 'Who would have thought,' he said at one point, 'that in this obscure place—' He broke off to consult the scroll map of the river. He looked at Yue: 'The white man must be stopped.'

'Stopped?' said Yue Fat. 'How?'

'He will know of his wife's theories. He is an equivalent danger and demands equivalent remedy. We must send the soldiers after him.'

Yue, his voice cracking with stress, said that the soldiers were useless – one old, one stupid, one a boy. And they were needed here, to guard the money.

'But if they are useless?' said Chang. 'It's a risk, but these are desperate times. And now I have an idea: we can say that we were robbed by the white man and his whore.'

'But I still need a bodyguard.' Yue Fat called for his shoes. He didn't put them on, however.

'Meanwhile we will take steps against the white woman,' said Chang. He spoke with an odd formality: 'There are many hazards in these hills, against which even the most cautious traveller cannot guard.'

'Absurd!'

'Perhaps the white woman could commit suicide, which is accounted a great shame among Christians. Either way she must vanish. And her horse of a husband will know of her theories, which could rouse the people like the lies of the Taiping. Already these whites have stirred up the fisher folk, who hate us.'

'Yes, yes, they do,' said Yue Fat. He saw why his secretary wasn't listening: Chang wanted to think that the white woman's theories threatened the Empire, and that the Empire would reward their suppression. Yue fiddled with his fan: 'Only do not harm her here. Not here.'

'And the man?'

'I don't care about the man,' said Yue with irritation.

'He might have an accident on the river, which is so hazardous to the inexperienced. We will say that he stole the Imperial tax money, and that he vanished with the fisher woman, that they fled together and have died together. It will be a satisfactory scandal.'

At last they agreed: the three soldiers would pursue the white man, taking the riverboat now moored at Market Village, and Grace would somehow be silenced.

'But we won't do anything here,' Yue said. 'We are surrounded by witnesses – the fisher folk.' He didn't mention Chang's desire to kill her.

'She is an embittered mongrel,' said Chang, 'and therefore especially dangerous, since her Chinese face gives weight to her barbarian superstition.' He imagined he was back in Canton. He was addressing a committee of officials, called to applaud his triumph. He raised his arm in a horrible habit acquired from the whites. 'She is the very symbol of the unwise intercourse of China and the foreigners.'

They argued for the rest of the day. Grace must be silenced, said Chang. But not here, said Yue, not here.

'I'm going into the hills,' said Grace.

She was again at the collector's door, but this time didn't linger. 'I have work of historical and religious importance.' Secretary Chang looked away to hide his surprise.

'I'll stay by the river, so I can't be lost. I have a little pack, with clothes and food. I'm quite capable.' She glanced at him. 'And there are dangers here.'

'The headman won't trouble you again.'

'The obvious answer is to invite me into the collector's house.'

'But didn't you know?' said Chang. 'The soldiers have already left on an Imperial mission: in their absence, my master can't adequately protect you.'

He added, 'We are very sorry about your difficulty,' but his sharp little tongue popped out to lick his lips, so that he seemed only professionally gentle, like a doctor with bad news.

Grace gave him a letter. 'This is for my husband. You'll give it to him, please. And perhaps you will safeguard our belongings.'

Chang bowed and put the letter in his sleeve. 'You can't go alone. Think of the danger. And you will need porters. I'll arrange this. And protection.'

She almost wept at this kindness, though no doubt he was false. She said, 'Do you believe that my husband and this woman . . .?'

Chang again looked away. 'There were rumours,' he said.

'Who will go with us?'

'The collector will be eager to help. The soldiers have other duties, which I have described, but there is otherwise no difficulty. I will go with you until you are clear of the village, and we will take an appropriate number of porters. We can be ready quickly.'

In the late evening John and Little Niece sat in the boat. They had pulled into a creek off the main river and were moored to a bush. Fields stretched into the dusk, but the peasants had gone, leaving rubbish smouldering in a ditch. From downstream came the roar of broken water, but here the river was straight and full, and its little tributary was so slow that green algae covered the water, and a man might be tempted to walk there.

Inland the creek was crossed by a pretty little bridge where houses crowded on either bank. John was dizzy after the river, but rowed to the houses, which seemed half sunk into the ground because creepers grew over them on straw ropes. The creepers had met over the narrow stream, and beans, loofahs, lentils and gourds hung from above, deepening the gloom. John and Little Niece sat unseen on the black water between the houses: oil lamps glimmered through paper windows and there was the sound of families.

He rowed a little further. Now they floated below a teahouse by the bridge, hearing murmured talk, the laughter of a woman selling sunflower seeds, and the song of birds which customers had brought, hanging their cages on the roof beams. The smell of opium drifted down from the teahouse hookah.

'We could stay here,' said Little Niece.

An old trader sat in the gloom, nodding in his boat tethered to the bank. John woke him with a hiss and bought peaches and a melon. Sick with tiredness, he rowed them back past the houses.

'They are cousins of the fisher folk, I think,' said Little Niece.

John rowed on, leaving a black trail swirling in the algae. Perhaps she could hear the roar of the river because she knelt in the boat and looked around, her face eager then fearful, though her beauty survived these changes like a word on a banner. 'We could stay here. In a little house with windows, and the teahouse near.'

'You could stay. I have to go back to my wife.'

'So instead we'll go downriver.'

'We'll start back upstream in the morning,' said John. 'We will go a little way on this boat, until the river is too fast, then we'll walk. Or perhaps we could go up on a riverboat: I have no more money, so perhaps I could be a deck coolie.' He tried to smile.

'We will go downriver, to where the spirits live,' she said, her face pale in the gloom. 'We will meet my parents, my brothers, and little Shen.'

They came again to the mouth of the creek. John climbed on to the bank and tied their prow rope to a bush as the moon freed itself from woods on the horizon. He was back in the boat when he frowned and said, 'Shen? But she is well.'

Little Niece began to open her coat. She stared at him without expression, pushing at the wooden buttons, her face pale as paper in the moonlight. He was taken by a great melting flood of desire. Her grubby fingers fumbled in the hessian. He saw her small breasts.

Then he frowned. Between her breasts was a bundle. It was held by a wide band of cloth wrapped round her waist. Was it a doll? Its grey face looked at him, scowling like a little old man.

'Oh, my Lord,' said John, because he recognized little dead Shen.

'She was well,' said Little Niece. 'She was well, then she fell asleep, and in the morning she was dead. So we will go downriver – you and I and little Shen. We will meet the Christian God and my family.'

John whispered, 'How did she die?'

'She was well and then she died. My husband would have sent her to the ghost world, and the aunts wanted to cut her up. So we will take her to the Christian heaven to be loved.'

John, gripping the boat, whispered, 'Did you kill her?'

'We will take her to the Christian heaven, to your home. We will go now. Let us go now.'

For a moment John pictured the heavenly city, its lights glowing on the water. 'We must go back,' he said, whispering against the vision.

John slept well. He dreamt he had fallen in the river, which at first was icy. The night was warm, however, so he grew easy in his dream until the water was as thorough as a lover, its fingers everywhere. He rolled with Little Niece, the river yielding like a quilt, until he saw they were being swept downstream and woke with a jolt.

He had slept late. Peasants were in the fields and a boat drifted in the shallows among staked nets, a man leaning over the side, his great hat shading the river as he looked for fish. Little Niece sat in the stern against the bright morning, watching him.

John stirred at once. Worried about his wife and nervous of Little Niece, he untied the mooring rope and pushed them from the shore.

'No,' said Little Niece. 'You have forgotten Shen.'

'If you want to put Shen in the river we can do it

now,' said John. In daylight he was inclined to be brutal. He poled them out into the river, pushing on the muddy bottom with the handle of his scoop. He reversed the scoop and began to scull upstream.

Little Niece grabbed his arm. He lifted her around the waist, feeling Shen, and carried her to the prow where he could watch her, though she was stiff in his arms and fearful.

The boat had spun in the current, so he turned them upstream again, keeping inshore because a riverboat was coming round the bend ahead. But they made poor progress from his sculling. He rested for a moment and watched the riverboat, its tillerman singing.

He moved amidships and tried paddling the boat like a canoe, but it was even worse. He had planned to hide the boat a little way upstream, where a bamboo grove came to the water's edge, but was already tired. If only there were oars.

He heard a shout. 'White barbarian!'

As he turned to the riverboat, Little Niece sprang into the water. He grabbed her ankle, and the boat tipped and wallowed as he leant over the side.

'White monster,' someone shouted. 'Leave her.'

John was pulling her ankle, but this drew her head below the surface. Instead he took her sleeve. She watched as if from a bed, then rolled from the jacket.

She began to sink. She looked up through the window of the water, Shen gazing from between her breasts. The child's lips moved and a bubble rose to the surface. It burst like a rebuke and with a start of guilt John leapt into the water. He kept a hand on the gunwale and groped into the depths for Little Niece, though the effort drew his face below the water.

Then he was shot in the head.

16

The sergeant had been content for once, chasing the Westerner downstream. Yue Fat's three soldiers had taken a riverboat from Market Village and the sergeant sat on their packs, piled in the low place near the stern. Occasionally he sent the young private to make tea at the charcoal stove or to question the crew, who had passed the white giant at a rapid. The youngster was shy and intense, and the two older men smiled as he stammered his questions.

It was good to get away from the settlement by the beach, where they were under the immediate gaze of Yue Fat and the girlish secretary, and where there were no taverns and no women except the stinking old fisher women and the pretty young one who had been taken by the giant.

'She will be useless to anyone else,' the sergeant called suddenly. The private was puzzled but then blushed. The corporal laughed.

The sergeant liked the river because downstream it passed Wuxuan, his ancestral homeland. His father had worked there in the magistrates' office, but worked harder at his poetry: he formed a reading circle for those who had passed only the basic Imperial examinations – clerks, pawnbrokers, book-keepers and others of the literate underclass. They drank wine, walked in the country, and discovered the writings of a local man, Hong Xiuquan, who declared that the Christian missionaries hadn't brought a new religion but had merely reminded China of its ancient god, who had been displaced by the follies of Buddhism, Taoism, and peasant superstition. Even China's king of the devils, Yan Luo, was the same serpent who had deceived Adam and Eve: Yan Luo was feared by the Chinese, but had been trodden by God because he was weak as bean curd, which seems solid but is full of water.

Then Imperial troops slaughtered Hong's converts among the peasants, who were crazed by a famine. The sergeant's parents had been amused by this creed which contradicted the classics, but now they joined Hong's rebels, who called themselves the Taiping, and marched north towards the capital.

Endless victories ensued, confirming god's support. They swept aside the corrupt Imperial army, its gunpowder stale from storage, its swords rusted into the scabbards, and the sergeant was born while the Taiping besieged Nanjing, which fell and became the rebel capital. Here he grew up, learning that Hong had been born of god's first wife before the creation of heaven and earth, and that he often returned to heaven where his organs had been changed for precious stones and gold, and where he was greeted by his brother Jesus and by Jesus's wife and five children – three boys and two girls. God, who had a golden beard and a high-brimmed hat, complained about the false doctrines of Buddhism and

Taoism and revealed that the people of heaven had whipped Confucius for his folly.

In the sergeant's eleventh year, Nanjing was besieged by Imperial troops. Soon there was no food and Hong declared that everyone should eat manna from heaven. No one knew how to obey this command, even though several laggards became 'Heavenly candles', being doused in lamp oil and set alight. So Hong called the people to watch him wandering the palace grounds gathering the manna, which to mortal eyes looked like weeds.

Women and children fled the city, impeded only by the gangs who robbed them, while the defenders buried barrels to the lips to listen for enemy tunnellers. Then they dug counterattacks, assaulting the Imperial tunnels with burning sulphur, bags of gunpowder or vats of sewage.

Too young to fight, the sergeant had sat in a listening barrel, cramped against a blind man who was thought thereby to have especially sharp ears. One day even the sergeant could hear the Imperial tunnellers, and scrambled out so that the defenders could breach the tunnel, fighting with one arm out of their sleeves to identify each other in the gloom. But the attackers had dug a second tunnel, and exploded a mine which killed dozens of Heavenly soldiers and cracked the city wall.

The blind man said that the city would fall and that its tunnellers were now digging away from the Imperial tunnels: they were still passing up soil, so nobody knew of their cowardice except the blind listeners. That night the sergeant crept into the abandoned tunnel, groping through sulphur fumes and the dismembered dead until he was in a long gallery lit by oil lamps. Imperial guards, crouched behind an earth bank, levelled arrows at his chest.

He had fallen to his knees, beating his head on the foul earth and declaring that he had no sympathy for the secondary red-haired devils in the city and believed in the true gods of China. Something in his wild gabble made the guards laugh, and he was allowed to crawl forward until they could spit on him and put their feet on his neck and see that he was only a child.

Still, children were the most fanatical of the god-worshippers, and one of the Imperial guards kicked him with relish, his thin lips drawn tight, and called him 'man with no ancestors' because he had drunk the Jesus medicine and his forefathers would wander uncomforted in the dark.

But the sergeant claimed to be a local villager enslaved by the Jesus worshippers. He was allowed to the surface where he dug trenches, carried stores and finally laid siege to his own city. He thought of his family inside, but saw only the scorched city walls hung with chamber pots and menstrual rags to drive off the evil spirits which inspired the enemy. The Imperial troops were not deterred, working their cannon all day and at night galloping round the city with barrels full of stones to multiply the sound of hooves. And night and day they tunnelled under the walls, beating drums to hide the sound of digging.

When the city fell he crept through the ruins, by now

a full Imperial soldier with the first of his matchlocks, and found his family dead. Hong, sodden with women, had ascended to his Father: his wives had hung themselves from trees above the grave, and his sons and tributary kings were killed as they fled south to their spiritual homeland by the river.

'I'm an old man,' the sergeant now thought. 'I have known too many stupid missions.' He spat into the water, thinking about Yue Fat and Chang, who were weak and therefore dangerous. He remembered his confusing instructions from the little secretary, who had talked of kidnap and rape and how the white man was an invader whose lies poisoned the Empire. Yue Fat had said nothing, though he was the civil authority. He watched from the best chair, red-faced as if regretting his last meal, his eyes wide apart like a cow's.

'You must free the fisher woman,' Chang said, 'even though the white man might resist, and even though extreme measures might be necessary, since the punishment for his crimes is well known.'

Then Chang wanted a guide into the mountains and had sent the sergeant to recruit headman Sho. But Sho was slumped under his hut and wouldn't talk. The sergeant, impatient in the stinking village, had seen Jivu Lanu the shaman preparing to go upstream. He distrusted Jivu, but hired him in revenge against Chang, who had issued unclear orders, which are the curse of every soldier.

For the same reason he had no wish to catch the barbarian. Let some other poor soldier find the giant, who couldn't hide in China, though he would be aided by the wild country, which a barbarian could better endure. With luck the white man would not be found, since he could hide in any creek or village and had several hours' start.

Still, the sergeant was irritated that the riverboat was travelling so fast. He had thought it would drift with the current, but instead the coolies chanted and sang, leaning on the oars until trees fled past like horses, and still the tillerman howled them on. As they moored for the night the captain said angrily that the boat had to go faster than the current or it couldn't be steered, but the sergeant didn't understand.

Next morning the young private was questioning the passengers who had embarked overnight. He felt the smiles of the older men as he struggled, and his anger transferred to the white barbarian. He stammered his questions at a fool of a coolie, torn between shyness and his passion to stop the long-nose. He thought of the headman's pretty wife and of the barbarian's great shoulders, spread like wings over her helplessness. The private trembled.

They had come to a stretch where the river was wide and calm, so the coolies took turns to visit the water barrel. The boat slowed accordingly, but the tillerman seemed content to scull. It was suddenly quiet, until the private shouted, 'White barbarian!'

The sergeant was dumbfounded. Large and clear and unmistakable, rowing upstream near the far bank, the white giant stood in the headman's boat.

The sergeant ran to the brazier and lit his fuse cord. The two boats drew level as he threaded the cord into his musket, angry at the white man's stupidity. The barbarian leant over the water, his white hair shining in the morning sun, the perfect target.

'White monster. Leave her,' shouted the private, and they saw Little Niece in the river.

Now the white man was at the far side of his boat. He was bending over the water, and the sergeant found that he couldn't shoot a man in the buttocks. 'Shit on your ancestors,' he muttered.

They had passed the barbarian, though the corporal shrieked at the tillerman to halt. Then John was in the river, and the sergeant crouched to aim. It was a difficult shot – everything moving, the white man shrunk to a tuft of hair. But the sergeant recalled how John had smiled at his musket. His aim tightened.

From a moving boat, at a moving target, his range increasing, the sergeant fired.

17

On their path up the river Grace halted many times, while secretary Chang twitched with irritation and Jivu Lanu smoked and stared at her.

Walking cleared her thoughts, and she marvelled that John would drift into this betrayal. But then she recalled the death of his old amah. Perhaps he wanted to return to Canton for the funeral, and believed that Grace would refuse him. But why had he taken Little Niece?

During such thoughts she stood on the track or leant against one of the great boulders. Once she put her forehead against a boulder, but this made her think of a woman weeping and brought the grief up her throat.

Secretary Chang had ceased his pretence of kindness. 'We should go on,' he would say in his cold voice. Grace had to carry her own pack, since Chang's promised porterage had shrunk to the shaman Jivu Lanu, who carried only his square medicine pack. Even Chang had a knapsack.

'Like a picnic,' he had said in English as they left the village, though he looked helpless in his silk gown and cloth shoes, so that Grace wondered what emergency had stripped the collector of his soldiers. Her own load included the Mission funds: perhaps the money clinked, but she didn't trust her senses and in any case couldn't adjust her pack under the eyes of her companions. Towards evening they looked down into a wooded valley. Scattered among trees were a dozen huts.

In a daze of misery she lay in a long building shared with three families and their tumbling brown children. Her two companions slept nearby among a rubble of household goods. Sometimes she thought, 'Perhaps it is a mad mistake. Why would John be so foolish?' But mostly her grief seemed deserved and her marriage a vanity.

She wrote: *As it is declared in Proverbs, 'the lips of a strange woman drop as an honeycomb, and her mouth is smoother than oil: But her end is bitter as wormwood, sharp as a two-edged sword. Her feet go down to death: her steps take hold on hell.'*

She did not explain this text, only writing: *Every woman is sometimes beautiful: it is a question of how often.* She had loved her husband's beauty but was punished through the beauty of Little Niece. Beauty is a word, the shape that speaks, but she would listen henceforward to the Word of the Lord.

She recalled her own desires and how such passions are stronger in a man, so that even the best could succumb, though later they are racked by guilt. She thought about the headman's silly idol, and how she had humiliated her husband, a thing that men detest. Perhaps her husband was wandering the hills, and her duty was forgiveness, to gather the stray into God. She would never ask about his actions, if only he returned and stayed and loved her.

With this thought she wept under her blanket, each sob very hard like a cough. She recalled her dormitory in

Hong Kong, and the blank bodies of the other children, their female parts like the lips of fishes. Her words were useless, outbid by that tongueless mouth, the wet book, belly speaking to belly.

Secretary Chang might have changed his plans about Grace, but was shocked by the hills. During their hasty departure, he had thought of taking her to the Yi slave-owners far upstream in the Cool Mountains. But such a journey was now inconceivable, nor could he stay in this squalid village. He decided again on murder.

First he asked about the links between China and Christianity. He made notes of her answers, because the more impressive her ideas, the more he would be praised for suppressing them. He trembled with fear and elation, picturing a tribunal in Canton where he showed the parallels between Grace's theories and the greatest calamity in Chinese history, the Taiping Rising, which had also begun on this river, its leader inspired by Prot-estant pamphlets handed out in the very Cantonese streets where the woman's husband had worked. Above all, the Taiping had likewise claimed that China once worshipped the Christian God.

He would kill her with aconite. Jivu had a tuber of the plant, which he had chopped with raisins to kill the daughter of Little Niece, and which – crushed with ginger juice, dragon's blood and wild sesame seeds – made a tonic for married men called The Tartar General Resumes the Battle. The same mixture was a potion 'essential for travel in these testing hills', as he explained to secretary

Chang, opening his pack and noting the little man's sudden excitement.

Jivu agreed a price for the poison, but grew suspicious. He held the root in a tongue of leather, noting how even its dust caused a tingling in his nose. He touched a fragment to his tongue and felt its *qi* as first fire and then numbness: later there were palpitations of the heart. Yet he told Chang that the tuber was old.

Irritated, Chang was drawn into unwise arguments with the woman, saying, 'We need no white man's God.'

'Instead you have hundreds of Chinese gods.'

'Yes, and so had no war of religion until Christians came, who have one God and are therefore intolerant.'

'Our God is the God of peace,' said Grace. 'This is what the Chinese will learn.'

'The Chinese?' cried Chang. '*You* are Chinese!' And he lifted his pigtail and pulled the corners of his eyes, to show how she resembled him. Her tireless words would soon be stilled, however, since aconite first paralyses the throat.

Yet there was no aconite. Jivu Lanu searched the hills, and at once found a handsome specimen, its purple blooms sprouting hip-high from a rocky crevice full of rabbit droppings. But he thought, 'The little secretary has no use for a woman: this is not true for proper men.'

'We have to go to the next village,' he told Chang. 'There is aconite there, further into the hills.'

Jivu Lanu had always been wild, because his birth involved ghosts, adultery and murder.

A year after she was driven away by the five men of the fisher folk, his mother had learnt that ill-luck attended her also. Her village, linked to the great civilization which outsiders called the Yi, was more prosperous than the wretched huts on the slope, and thus drew travellers. One brought smallpox, which killed half her clan and fixed her in a mask of scabs. She lay next to baby Jivu, knowing that if she died he would be buried with her, or their bodies left for the dogs.

Instead she recovered a little and crawled to the thorn bush which the villagers had tied in her doorway. Through its branches she saw her mother condemned as a witch, who had fired disease arrows from her eyes and must be buried under the coffin of one of her victims.

Perhaps these things were responsible for Jivu's mad moods, which often left her in a pool of blood. When he was sixteen, her neighbours helped to drive him from the house. He was her only child, and should support her, but instead she had lived on the poor crops which the crows left in her field, small as a garden. She expected no different because the children of shamans were notoriously unstable: Jivu was too close to the ghost world and infected by its creatures.

For a few months he was a porter along the valley, carrying salt, hemp, grain and straw sandals, and spending his wages in the tavern. He learnt to say nothing about his own problems, which were laughed at, but after every misfortune in the villages – a sick animal or a broken axle – he reminded the elders how his father had been a powerful shaman who was murdered by the five strangers in the next valley.

At last the local shaman held an exorcism at the pothole where Jivu's father had been thrown and where his ghost presumably loitered, crazed with anger, blasting the settlement of the men who had killed him and the valley of the woman who had caused the murder.

'I give you heaps of boiled grain,' the exorcist said. 'If you don't believe this, count them.' But among the grains were mustard seeds, which are too small to count, so that the ghost was bewildered and then defeated.

Perhaps afterwards there was less ill-luck in the valley, yet Jivu still suffered the humiliations of youth, no doubt because he had failed to avenge his father. He went to the village of the five murderers and found that his father's hand was heavy upon it: only a naked old man remained, his grey face blinking from a hut the size of a coffin. Jivu crept through the wrecked village, ensuring they were alone, then sat on a log to watch him.

The old man was lonely and happy to talk, but had a shrivelled leg and ulcers through to the bone and became confused, calling Jivu by the names of the living and dead. He told the short history of the settlement, and how a shaman had cuckolded his friend and been murdered, and how his friend had gone back downstream. He whispered anxiously about the fish god, and described his home village at the pebble beach. Jivu Lanu gave him poisoned beans and carried off some rusty tools in a rusty cooking pot.

Then he felt the stirrings of the spirits, especially when drunk. He couldn't be taught the tribal magic, however, since his father hadn't been a Yi, though a local healer permitted him to buy the tasteless barley beer and taught him the chant for exorcism, in which Jivu could claim an interest. They sat in the tavern, heads together, while Jivu learnt the words and drew maps in spilt drink on the bench between them, tracing the path of dead souls along the river's windings to Hong Kong.

Jivu liked the Yi proverbs about revenge. Hoping his father's ghost would hear, he told the shaman, 'We do not forget an enmity, as a fir joint does not rot,' and, 'If the son is strong he will avenge the father, if he is very strong he will avenge the grandfather,' and, 'A horse's strength is in his haunch, an ox's strength is in his neck, and a man's strength is in his clan.'

Then the shaman had said, 'You have no clan,' and Jivu thereafter drank alone, sitting on a low bench against the wall, thinking about the *qi*, which moved rivers, directed procreation and digestion, carried dead souls downstream, and made a tree of blood through the generations of a family, though he was the only man in the valley who couldn't recite his ancestry.

One night the landlord was talking to his daughter. They sat in the far corner, smoking their pipes among the earthenware jugs. As they laughed, they sometimes glanced at their only customer. This was no more than their job, so they were angry when Jivu Lanu threw the bench at them.

The landlord grabbed the seat of Jivu's pants, pulling

them upwards to squeeze his testicles, and thus propelled him into the river. Jivu crawled from the water with a broken wrist, but then was lucky, encountering an old woman who indulged his pretensions because she was lonely. In her house he began his career as a shaman, at first tentative as if expecting a prohibition, then visiting neighbouring families, who gave him food. The old woman grew jealous and claimed the food as rent. Tired of her complaints he began his wanderings.

He believed that he could charm wild animals to offer their throat to his knife, but had no success and instead ate wild plums and loquats, or crept to farms at night to take plums, pears, cabbage hearts and red turnips, or opened the sluices of paddy fields, listening for the struggles of cultivated fish as they choked on the mud.

One night his back was pocked with lentils from a farmer's shotgun. He lay all night in a cabbage field and towards dawn he wept because there was no one to take out the pellets. Jivu was jealous of the gun because there were no firearms in his home valley, and warriors still wore feathers and buffalo-hide armour. At a fireworks factory he watched the mixing of gunpowder, and sat on hillsides aiming a stick at distant animals, imagining he could send death from afar. He met a woman and child on a high path and took food and a cloak, though without much violence, later thinking how he might have stroked the woman with the point of a gun.

Instead he was trapped by bandits, against whom his poverty was no defence since even beggars have a liver to steal. But Jivu pretended leprosy and by the time the lie was discovered had interested them with talk of the ghost world. Their ponies bit off faces, yet he held their tails as the bandits trotted up mountain tracks after lone travellers: he scavenged with the women for the last rags and hair.

He escaped the bandits and begged in market towns, where he met a healer with a square wooden pack like a cupboard. Inside were shelves and drawers which were full of paper parcels, bamboo cylinders, and jars of leather, glass and pottery. Jivu volunteered to be the healer's servant and protector, and travelled with him for a summer, learning the uses of radish as an expectorant, lotus as an aphrodisiac, cow's cud which would certainly have cured the cholera which killed the fisher folk, and grass from the grave of a woman dead in childbirth, which prevents an infant crying or perhaps ensures a parent's deafness. He could apply mosses whose virtue lay in the place of their gathering, whether roofs, privies, wells or the bottoms of boats, and used accordingly for different wounds, and could mix a tablet called the Plum Flower Lozenge, made of bean curd, woman's milk and toad's spittle.

There were two further tablets – one called the Pill of the Seven Precious Handsome Whiskers and another called Helping the Yin and Bringing Back the Soul – whose contents he didn't learn before the healer denounced him. His hand on Jivu's shoulder, addressing a bustling market behind the magistrate's office in a riverside town, the healer said that if he vanished or was murdered, especially if Jivu was found with his pack, the town should remember and avenge him.

Jivu had indeed planned to steal the pack, but had not decided how. He waited outside the town at dusk and followed the healer to his camp, killing him with a stone as he slept. It was a clumsy murder, far from the river, to which he spent two nights dragging the body. In a later year he returned to the riverside town: he had the pack but was not molested, so perhaps the healer had fewer friends than he thought.

Along with the medicine he had learnt the concepts of Wind and Water, and combined these Chinese skills with Yi tradition, feeling himself a superior type of shaman, ready like his father to cuckold the dull husbands of the peasant women. He pictured his father, grave and patient, listening as the women talked of their woes, then laying his strong hands upon them in the bushes. But Jivu Lanu was bored by the plain wives and nervous of the pretty ones. On hot nights in the hills he stood naked and felt he could run all night through the parting darkness. The *qi* filled his penis and he said, 'Little brother, when will we find a woman?' and almost wept with longing.

Unsatisfied, he travelled downstream. When he found the village of the fisher folk, he understood why he had no woman. It was connected with the journey which all ghosts make to the sea. When we sicken and die we no longer have strength to resist the flow of the *qi* and are swept downstream to the afterworld. Only a person who dies while strong, perhaps in an accident or by murder, can fight the *qi* and stay to trouble the living. His father was such a hungry ghost but had died in a pothole, from which his ghost, driven off by the exorcism, should have slid helplessly away – through underground brooks, out of springs, along tributaries, and thence down the great river, slippery as a gut, to melt into the ocean at Hong Kong.

But here was the difficulty. The tribal exorcism had surely forced the ghost on its final journey, but during its passage downstream it had come to the village of the fisher folk, where for once the river slowed. Perhaps it had first noticed the collector, for ghosts love money, and nowhere upstream was there such silk and silver as a tax collector owns. Then perhaps it saw Market Village, for markets are a playground for ghosts, who finger the goods and rustle the coins in the pockets of traders.

Sooner or later, though, it had smelled its own blood. It saw that the fisher folk were related to those who had thrown it to drown in the dark. No hungry ghost could miss such a chance for revenge – and his father's ghost was especially powerful. It had blocked the flow of *qi*, causing an accumulation of destructive energy, while reaching upstream so that Jivu pined for women until he could weep.

But Jivu had confronted his father's ghost and already his luck had changed. Soon he would be alone with Grace.

18

The day after he shot John, the sergeant was drinking in a riverside tavern. He was arguing with a raftman about whether the river dragon faced the mountains or the sea.

The raftman had just arrived from a logging camp in the mountains. Strapped to his raft, a mat shelter on his back, with a long pole to lever past rocks and rapids, he had ridden a vicious tributary of the river, and couldn't stop, even at nightfall. Dizzy with opium and the spinning of the raft as it raced downriver out of control, he had shot through rapids which might invert him and past cliffs undercut by the river, where his raft might be pinned for ever like the good-luck posters glued to a doorframe at New Year.

Here, where the river was docile, his raft would be bound with dozens of others for the journey to the coast. Tomorrow he would start his journey back, creeping overland at night like an eel because everyone hated the raftmen, whose craft slowed as they entered the downstream stretches but still came on as ponderous as battering rams, tipping river folk into the water where they were torn between saving their boat or striking out for the raft to kill its pilot.

Now the raftman was drunk, and told the sergeant

loudly that the river dragon had its head in the mountains: water flowed downwards through the dragon and was pissed out into the ocean. The dragon's scales therefore faced downstream, which was why upstream travel was difficult; it also irritated the dragon, so that raftmen travelled back to the mountains on foot.

The sergeant pointed out that the river grew smaller towards the mountains, as a dragon dwindles towards the tail: upstream travel was therefore pleasing and comfortable to the dragon, who liked his scales to be stroked, and so the raftman should find a boat to carry the sergeant and his men back upriver.

It was funny to make the raftman thump the table, but the sergeant didn't mind travelling further downstream to find a riverboat, because it would keep him away from the boring fisher folk village. It also gave time for the white man to die.

Ignoring the sergeant's orders, their riverboat captain had steered them to where John floated with a bullet in his head. He was too heavy to lift from the river, so the coolies held his arms while he snored and choked in the water, nuzzled by the drowned body of Little Niece, which vanished when the riverboat slowed at the raftmen's camp. The camp was so wild that riverboats didn't stop there, and the three soldiers had to leap from the moving boat onto the muddy bank beside the foreigner.

It was a fine conundrum for the sergeant as he stared at the great figure stretched on an ash heap while the raftmen wondered about stealing the colossal sandals. The sergeant checked John's wound and laughed, calling his men to see how well he had aimed. The slug had struck the back of the head, slightly to one side, but slowed by the water so that it hadn't pierced the skull, instead travelling around the head under the scalp, and could now be felt above the giant's ear.

The corporal shivered as he touched the barbarian's hair, soft as rabbit fur, but found the slug under its quilt of scalp and said, 'Fine shooting, your honour.' The sergeant smiled, as if such shots were commonplace in his career. He patted his musket and said, 'Old but excellent,' and they all laughed, knowing that he saw himself in the weapon.

Then the sergeant stood back with a smile. He told his soldiers, and a gathering circle of raftmen, about clever bullets which had entered at the shoulder and left at the knee, or had burst from the skin in the shape of a coin or a shower of needles, or had thrown out a bone like a fish leaping from a stream, or were found among broken teeth in a dead man's mouth and used again, or had knocked off a conscript's jaw, the man refusing to die, his tongue lolling like a dog's as he sat stunned at the campfire or marched bewildered with his comrades, who were at first solicitous but then made jokes and at last grew silent to devise his death.

A raftman had glanced at the barbarian and said, 'This one also refuses to die.'

Secretary Chang and his party had moved further into the hills. They were staying with villagers who gave names to the trees which bent above their huts, and dressed them with beads and feathers, and took only their dead branches for firewood. Occasional tigers traversed the forest, so the village children stepped directly from the stilted houses into the arms of the nearer trees.

The village pigs, however, took their chances on the ground. They scavenged in the forest and ate the excrement that dropped from the huts. But this procedure was an agony for secretary Chang.

One morning Jivu Lanu saw him get up in the greyness of dawn. Fearing treachery, he watched the little man let down the bamboo ladder, cross into bushes and lift his skirts.

The largest sow approached, but Chang had a stick. Crouched in the undergrowth, his stick raised, the pig circling and snorting, Chang cast embarrassed glances towards the huts.

But Jivu Lanu was the only witness to this comedy, and watched unseen. He didn't smile. He had been contemplating a drastic act, which now seemed more possible.

John woke, then slept, then woke again. At some point he listened to the gossip of Yue Fat's soldiers, and wondered how they had come to him. The pain was a great growth on the side of his head: its roots crossed his face, which burned with a fever.

Then he was blinking at an oil lamp. He was in a hut, soldiers and peasants peering down at him in the dim light. He pulled himself up and sat against a wall. There seemed to be grit between his teeth or in the hinge of his jaw: plates of bone cracked in his head.

He stood up in stages, pain roaring over him like a waterfall. He swayed above the soldiers, then stepped over someone's legs and blundered outside. It was very dark, and he waited till he could see the dim outline of sky. The hills swung around him so he put a hand on the hut, which flexed under his fingers.

He was standing in a village yard. Other houses surrounded the yard, their lamplight shining in rooms full of comfortable people. Their doors were open, he realized, because the air was warm. He must have come to the lowlands, but couldn't see how, unless he had slept for a week.

He tottered across the yard, which was paved with bamboo mat, and leant against a pig pen. The smell of hot iron wafted from a forge. He looked back at the hut where he had been held. The sergeant stood in its doorway, watching him calmly.

He crossed to the blacksmith's, walking like a careful drunk. Inside, a lean man sat by a forge, which was cooling after his toil. He looked up at John, too tired to be surprised.

John said: 'What is the name of this village?'

'The name?'

'Where is it? Is it near the river?'

The blacksmith smiled. 'Very near,' he said.

The three soldiers appeared in the doorway. 'Why did you murder Little Niece?' said the sergeant.

John pushed past him and walked into the darkness, the soldiers not troubling to follow. He left the circle of houses and saw what seemed a flat plain stretching to the hills, which had resumed their movement against the stars. He took a few steps, then fell heavily.

The matting which covered the village yard had suddenly ended. In its place were gnarled rocks, or mossy boulders, or hard earth ridged by ploughing. It was inexplicable, and he knelt while pain beat against his head.

A ripple passed under him. It was like an earthquake perhaps, this lifting and falling of the ground. Another ripple passed, and he understood where he was and why the soldiers didn't fear his escape.

Jivu Lanu said that the little secretary had returned to Yue Fat. Grace thought that there was perhaps more safety with two men than one, but was preoccupied, pondering the theology of betrayal.

She wrote: *The Israelites wandered for 40 years in the wilderness, surrounded by heathens and the gods of heathens. Again and again God warned them, saying, 'Ye shall not go after other gods, of the gods of the people which are round about you, lest the anger of the Lord thy God be kindled against thee.'*

Instead, said the Lord, 'Ye shall overthrow their altars, and break their pillars, and burn their groves with fire; and ye shall hew down the graven images of their gods, and destroy the names of them out of that place.'

But if they made 'the likeness of any beast that is on the earth, the likeness of any winged fowl that flieth in the air, the likeness of any thing that creepeth on the ground, the likeness of any fish that is in the waters beneath the earth . . . I call heaven and earth to witness that ye shall soon utterly perish'.

And God was right to suspect the Israelites, who indeed broke their word and went whoring after other gods and served Baal and Ashtaroth and Asherah, bowing to a golden calf even as Moses received the Ten Commandments on the summit of Mount Sinai.

She laid her pen aside. She would not record how the same fate had befallen her husband, who had also journeyed among heathens, and how the doom of the Lord had been fulfilled: their little mission was wrecked, and John wandered in the desolation of the absence of the Lord, who had said, 'Yet ye have forsaken me, and served other gods; wherefore I will deliver you no more. Go and cry unto the gods which ye have chosen; let them deliver you in the time of your tribulation.'

So she thought how her husband had betrayed God, but not of his other betrayal.

Next morning John felt better. He went outside, his head jarring with every step, and confirmed they were on an enormous raft.

It was a bright warm morning, with a cool breeze from the river. Moving his head with care he stared along the great craft, its logs stirring so that it seemed some hybrid of river and land.

He had seen such rafts near Canton, drifting on the slack current. But the river here was as fast as a running man. And it had widened as he slept, a grey plain under the heat haze, its banks a distant blur. A swimmer would drift for miles, weakening in the icy water, before he reached the shore, which might be too steep for a landing, especially if the swimmer had a bullet in his head.

The soldiers were watchful, befitting his purposeful state. They wore their bamboo armour, but the sergeant didn't have his musket. 'The best of both worlds,' thought John.

He walked among the wooden houses, careful with his pain like a man with a tray, the sergeant at his elbow, the two soldiers trailing behind. Goats watched blandly. A flood of chickens parted around them. The pig pen spread its smell across the raft.

The sergeant explained how Little Niece had been taken by the river, and John sat on a bale of mountain cotton, sick with pain and sorrow. He said, 'And my wife?'

'She is well, of course. We are going back. You will accompany us. You will see your wife.' As he spoke, the sergeant looked for the little bump of the bullet over John's ear. The white man would need further help to enter the world of ghosts. At the next big town they would leave the raft, conveyed ashore by its rowing boat. They would walk a little way along the river, and find a quiet place for murder.

The barbarian didn't seem angry at being shot – it was the strange humility of a prisoner – and of course he was weakened by his injury. Nevertheless, the soldiers sat close as John explored the matted blood at the back of his head, and the bruise around to his ear.

At noon the raft began to bustle. Men at its corners heaved at their oars, and the rowing boat set off towards the bank, its crew feeding a bamboo cable into the river. The cable stretched back to the raft, where it was fixed to a capstan. The soldiers were puzzled by a crewman standing in the middle of the rowing boat, steadying a basket as tall as himself.

John, grown wise from his weeks with the fisher folk, was looking downstream. A dark shape came swiftly around a bend in the river. It was an island, long and bare, with a ridge of rocks along its back like the bristles on a hog. Its sharp headland pointed at the raft.

The rowing boat was a little ahead of the raft and halfway to the shore. Its crew manhandled the huge basket over the side. At once, back on the raft, men began to chant and shout as they raced around the capstan, drawing in the great basket on its cable.

'What is this?' said the sergeant with a smile.

'It's a sea anchor, you fool,' John said in English. 'As the basket is pulled towards the raft, it pulls the raft from the path of that island, which I won't point to or even look at.' Scowling, he spun on his heels and took two steps towards the rear of the raft. Then he ran at full speed and leapt into the river.

It was still icy. Stunned, he hung underwater, the grey light feeble above him, his head cracking, then broke the surface. He squinted through his pain and saw the young private shrieking at the edge of the raft.

John swam towards the midstream, then rolled on his back, kicking with his sandaled feet, staring back at the raft. The private was dancing his indignation. Then, arms and legs flailing, he jumped into the river.

'He will drown,' thought John.

He kicked again, helped by anger. He had felt guilty about Little Niece, he realized, and hadn't questioned the soldiers' right to shoot him. But of course he would not stay with them.

He was on course for the island. He rested and looked back. The raft was drawing away, pulled by the current and the sea anchor. The young soldier thrashed in the waves, but the bare arm of the river had slid around his face. His comrades watched from the raft as he weakened in his sodden armour.

John turned and swam again, until the riverbed kicked his heels. He was dragged over rocks and gravel and could neither swim nor walk in the swift shallow water. A boulder jarred his hip and he held its slimy face. He gathered his breath as the river tugged his shoulders.

He crawled into the shallows and stayed for a time on hands and knees, the water making shackles round his wrists. The raft had vanished into the heat haze: no one was coming for him. He waded ashore, resting for some uncertain time in the lee of a rock. He closed his eyes, inside with the pain. He thought of the young soldier, helpless in the river's wrestler's grip, drifting with Little Niece towards Canton.

John was sheltered from the wind but exposed to the warm sun. He was wearing only his sandals, shirt and trousers, but soon recovered from the icy water. He smelt the tropics – dust, humidity from the river, the luxurious green. This was home, he thought, not the cool of the highlands.

He stood, pain throbbing with his pulse. It was mid-afternoon and he was too weak to leave the island. He must look for shelter.

He crept along the shore, over little headlands and gravel coves, the pain making him hunch, like the low roof in the headman's house. A shadow hung in his field of vision, high and to the right. It had been there, he realized, since he was shot.

He was near the downstream end of the island. He smelt wood smoke, though even this had to struggle past his hurt. He looked across the river for its source, but saw nothing. He stole forward, then hid among rocks.

The houses were on stilts, like the houses of the fisher folk. A man stood fishing from rocks and a youngster wielded a bamboo scoop in the shallows, but most of the villagers worked the land, bent-backed over seedlings on a swath of brown mud at the downstream end of the island.

He walked unsteadily to the houses. He sat against one of the stilts while the villagers eyed him. Someone brought water. A leaf with a smear of porridge was put at his side. He ate through the long afternoon, moving his jaw slowly because it hurt so much. An old man, too frail to work, sat beside him.

'Can I stay tonight?' said John in Cantonese.

'The giant is welcome,' said the man, giggling.

The old man helped him stand, and a circle of women watched as he crept up a creaking ladder. He entered a cool house and lay with a groan on its bamboo floor. There seemed no refuge from the pain and no position that gave ease. Only to stay still and quiet was a comfort.

He drifted in and out of sleep as the old man chattered about the village, which would soon be washed away in the spring floods as the villagers killed the pigs and loaded their mat shelters into the boats. Thereafter they would live for months on the water, fishing over the bare stilts of their village, mooring at night to the island's rocky peaks.

John saw the village underwater, dappled with light like the light through trees. In his dream, though, the pigs were alive. Children played in underwater silence, and the old man welcomed him to the village, bubbles rising from his smile.

The river fell in autumn, said the old man, leaving new mud in the island's lee. They planted winter wheat, and in spring they grew peas, beans, rice and cabbage. Often they were flooded before the harvest was in, but the mud was rich so there was always food from the year before. Anyway, their drowned crops brought fish to their fields, where all summer they cast their nets.

John saw the villagers in the drowned fields. They were graceful as river weeds, and fishes twisted through their legs like cats. Little Niece beckoned from one of the houses, because under the river such things were not forbidden.

Grace woke suddenly thinking, 'Dagon.'

She turned to the book of Judges and read again the

story of this fish god of the Philistines, to whose temple Samson was brought, and how he pulled down its pillars and crushed himself and the heathens, and of the parallels with John, her great man, who had gone to the altar of the fish god and thus destroyed their mission.

She thought of fish, the speechless creatures, and of the time when 'the earth was without form and void, and darkness was upon the face of the deep'. She wondered about that black ocean before the making of light and land, and about what had swum there, and had survived the Flood, and survived still.

19

John sat in the sun all morning, leaning against a house stilt and staring over the brown water, which could carry him swiftly to Canton. He was drowsy, and wondered if the old man had given him medicine. He recalled tumbling in his fever, but had then entered a deeper sleep.

Towards noon the old man's son rowed him from the island. John had found a twist of tobacco in his trouser pocket, and gave him half, but had no way of asking how far they were from the pebble beach.

He walked all day, the river bank level and dry and the pain in his head growing less, though his sight was troubled by the shadow. It was dark when he reached a coolie village.

The village was made of matting, and its brothels, taverns and opium dens would be moved up the valley side as the river rose. Half a dozen boats were moored at the bank, and he stood in each circle of lamplight asking if they were going upstream and needed a willing hand who would work without pay. But they stared at the white monster with open mouths and only said, 'We do not, we do not.'

In the last boat a fat woman was berating her coolies. They had shrunk to a lump of brown flesh in the stern, but one of them pointed at John, as if to distract her.

John was asking his questions when the woman cried, 'Yes, my crew is useless. Anyone must be better.'

She blinked with surprise as he stepped aboard. Gruffly she told the coolies to give him food, since he could do more work than all of them.

John squeezed among the coolies, gulping cold porridge as they arranged themselves to sleep, curling together like dogs on the bare boards, with the friendliest whispers about the bulk of their new shipmate, about the captain's wife who had scolded them, and about her husband, who watched over his opium pipe.

John fell asleep at once, but was troubled by rats which stirred under the bilge-boards then searched the boat, scandalizing the captain's hens in their cage on the roof, and jumping to the deck to hunt among the coolies, one dropping on him like a shoe. He half woke and found that the water was trying to speak. He strained to hear, as a parent strains for a child's first words, then dreamt he was drowning in the river again, its tongue in his throat.

Next day he could rest. They were under sail, and the captain leant all day on a greasy stain on the port rail, staring over the river as he tugged a whisker, glossy as wire, which sprang from a wart on his chin. John crouched with the coolies, who occasionally leapt to trim the mat sail but otherwise crowded in the stern, ducking as the tiller passed over them, and abusing the tillerman, who was a promoted coolie and could think of no answer except, 'Shit on your ancestors!'

John sat with his head drooping over the side where

the waves slapped like fish. The river was calmer down-stream, he decided, because its *qi* had been taken by fish and riverside crops and by the people who ate them. Then sunlight splintered on the surface and he looked away.

In the evening they moored at a small town, the river wide between low hills clothed in bamboo and locust trees. The captain's wife tended the household shrine and John eyed the candle and hoped that Song Lan's ghost would take a segment of its glow. He shivered, because Grace had found him at the headman's altar.

The captain cursed when an officer collected a toll on their cargo of salt, and again when lepers paddled little boats among the moorings, their begging baskets on poles. He rose in the night to fire his pistols, boats having crowded tight around them until a thief might step aboard. But rats were not discouraged: they probed like hands among the coolies and nibbled the skin from their heels.

The captain suffered these vexations to hire a pilot. In the morning his wife raised a bamboo hat on a long pole, and a solid capable man was chosen from the Masters of the Shallows who came with heavy dignity to compete for the work.

The moorings were crowded and there was no room to work the oars. John clambered over the logjam of boats to drop their anchor into clear water, and the captain's wife rewarded him with a cup of her boiled water. He joined the coolies to haul on the anchor rope until they were clear of the moorings, but must then satisfy himself from their keg of river water, with a bite of onion to clean it. The shadow hung in the right of his vision, pulsing with his heart.

Now the rapids began. At first they were low as a threshold, mere steps in the riverbed, the water combed smoothly over them with no foam. The giant raft had taken them without a quiver, but the boat noticed every one. It tipped and wedged like furniture in a stairwell, its prow fixed as the corner of a house, grinding on the rocks.

All day John and the crew jumped into the numbing water, heaving at wooden runners on the sides of the boat while the captain's wife scattered burning paper on the stream and murmured in a breathless hurry to her god or gods, breaking off to shriek at the coolies. Other rapids would be visible ahead, before the river curved, hiding the troubles to come.

Between their spells in the water, John and the coolies sat panting on the deck, staring at the pilot, whose silence invited inspection. He wore a cotton coat, a skullcap decorated with beads, and baggy trousers bound with tapes at the ankles. An apprentice sat cross-legged at his heels, passing tea or a fan or a pipe of tobacco. The pilot stretched out his right fist: his little finger was raised to indicate starboard, his index finger meant 'Steady', and his thumb meant port. He drank from the spout of his teapot, but his gaze never left the river. He stroked his chin, meaning that the stones would soon have white beards, meaning that big rapids were coming.

The captain's wife had been unsure of John, but soon

forgot herself so that he was berated like the rest: but he was called whenever he could lean his great weight on the runners, cloth around his blistered hands, pain cracking his head, distracted by his feet that turned the water like a plough, and the river rustling like pages or like disordered clothes, until the woman's voice roused him.

After one such outburst he waded to the bank, despite the shouts of the coolies who now relied on him. He strode ahead boldly, enjoying his solitude, only shared with the shadow of his pain. It was a clear warm day. He was on an inside curve of the river, the ground firm and level, laid down by the tame waters, and at first he outpaced the boat. But the river tightened like a whip before it cracks. Now he was on an outside curve and climbing a steepening slope, the bank becoming a cliff below him.

Still he climbed, pushing through bushes, glimpsing the boat outstripping him, while the shadow pulsed ahead. Far below the coolies laughed, lying on their backs and kicking their feet in the air, pretending to puff their pipes as he struggled on the slope, until the captain's wife slapped them back to their oars. At the next rapids he waded aboard, the vessel having refused to stop. His vision seemed misaligned, as if in a cracked mirror or because one eye was underwater.

Most difficult were the nights. Despite his pleas, the captain would not go on, even though moonlight lay on the broad waters. Then the river glittered in lizard scales, or in diamonds like a dog's tongue, or was ridged like a radish grater, or particulate as rice cake, or was like the wall behind the kitchen cupboard in the Mission House in Canton, which glistened with roaches which his amah had called 'the kitchen god's horsemen' and had secretly fed.

These visions drove him from the boat, because he had to hurry upstream where the river's nature would be clear. He would walk all night, he decided, and find a fresh boat in the morning. Hours later, having blundered through fields and ditches, his shirt torn, he was back on board.

Next day they passed the settlement of the raftmen, cruising under full sail, and at once there were serious rapids. The first seemed another aberration of the eyes. He frowned upstream, his head tipped, because the light on the water was wrong. The river bulged towards them, and only when he joined the coolies to uncoil the great bamboo tow-rope could he decipher the sloping water and its busy glitter.

Now they only came to the boat to eat and sleep. Each morning John hitched himself to the tow-rope, dizzy on a handful of rice and fried vegetables, but the coolies sang as they hauled. Their only covering was a cotton loop around their shoulders, and their nakedness had grace while they were strung out like figures on a Grecian frieze. But when the boat grew stubborn they dropped to their hands, scrabbling for purchase over the slithering gravel and humped boulders, gross as dogs.

Each evening the captain's wife struck a gong and they tied up. After another harangue the coolies crouched in the stern, scratching each other's backs, their faces twisted in bliss. They knew he was joining his wife in the mountains. One night, while John splashed river water against his head, they began sniggering: one of them whispered that if white women have larger eyes then no doubt they have larger mouths, and also larger – here they declined to continue.

John's Meerschaum pipe had somehow survived in his trouser pocket, although the stem was snapped, and the half-plug of good Cavendish was finally dry. He laid the splintered stem between his lips and applied a cinder from the stove, recalling the smashed boat they had seen that morning, planks and people swept down from a rapid. Clinging to a rock among the foam, more wretches cried for help, though they must have known that no one would provoke the water spirits with a rescue. Seeing John gave them new hope. 'Barbarian devil, save!' they called, but he could spare them hardly a glance as he rowed. The captain's wife looked with satisfaction at the wreck, as if fools and idlers had been punished.

He sucked down tobacco smoke, sour after its wetting. How wonderful was the relief, and how suddenly possible that with decent effort and Christian endeavour he might reach his wife.

He was thrown to the deck. The coolies had pitched him on his back, the captain's wife shrieking. He was sickened by the pain to his head, and at last the coolies brought him water. He had offended the river god, they said, having spat over the side.

Next morning the captain spent 250 chen on fireworks to appease the god. He also drove off the pilot, who (said the captain's wife) had engineered their halt to buy opium for sale downriver. In this bad atmosphere John left the boat, climbing over the side after breakfast, careful as a man in a tall hat, dropping to the muddy bank where their fireworks still smouldered and the first traders had come with food and charcoal. He didn't look back as the captain's wife shrieked and the coolies laughed.

The track at once turned inland. The low ground was damp among willows, but rose past fields of rice and tobacco towards a cleft in the hills. The shadow across his vision seemed faded: perhaps it was only an inability to move his eyes up and to the right. From the crest of the pass he saw the river ahead.

He was on a stretch of old Imperial road. Its paving slabs were tipped and jumbled, so he was glad when the unmade road resumed. He remembered how Grace had talked about China's decline: perhaps it was not so normal that a nation should squat among the crumbling wonders of its ancestors.

Jivu Lanu was telling Grace about his fight with the missionaries upstream. 'Stupid,' she said, 'Stupid.'

He stamped on the path to show how he had trodden the leaflets, and bit his sleeves because his wolf spirit had bitten Jesus.

'Do you think our Lord is afraid of a silly wolf,' said Grace, 'when he has harrowed hell and routed legions of devils?' She was sitting on a rock, her arms folded.

Jivu Lanu's dance became more serene and smooth,

with sliding leg movements and flowing hands, which he watched admiringly. For the moment he was inhabited by the crocodile.

'No one can fight my spirits,' he said.

20

It was night when John rounded the bend in the river-bank and came again to the beach of the fisher folk. The Mission House was dark, but he hurried up the slope and entered by the kitchen door. Moonlight streamed through the windows. He crept into the bedroom whispering, 'Grace, Grace.'

The house was bare. Only smears of spilled flour remained of their goods. The money was gone.

He hurried down to the beach. He climbed the head-man's ladder, but Sho held his door closed and shrieked insanely. John said, 'Where is my wife?' There was no answer, though John shouted again and again, shaking the ladder until the hut rocked.

An aunt spoke from the darkness: 'The white stranger must be careful if he visits the collector.'

Yue Fat sat among wreckage. Last night he had heard the Mission House being ransacked. Later there were drunken celebrations in the fisher folk village. He was in bed when he too was attacked.

Four people had burst in, their faces wrapped in rags. He had struggled but then sat quietly while one kept a hand on his shoulder and the others searched the house. They left with his personal goods, but didn't find his money. He told himself that he didn't know them, but the smell of fish had been too strong. Yet how could he report that he had sent away his bodyguard and then been robbed by women?

Yue Fat had lived in the little wooden house for nearly two years. At first he had painted and written poetry and practised his calligraphy, but was soon sick with boredom.

At the end of the first season, Imperial soldiers had come for the tax money. They had singing birds in brass cages, new waxed paper on their umbrellas, and Winchester repeating rifles which Yue Fat's sergeant examined with scepticism. The Imperial officer, whose sleeves were embroidered with silver, asked about the bandit Chang Tak Meng. Yue had heard of him: travellers had told his bodyguard about a drunken gang upstream that managed clumsy rapes and murders, staggering around village squares with clubs and mattocks. Yue Fat, a little irritated, said that such criminals required resources he did not have: here the officer bowed and indicated his men.

Yue Fat travelled with the soldiers for a week, watching from his sedan chair while the bandits were cornered in a cave and smoked out with a fire of gunpowder, sulphur and pepper. They swayed drunkenly as they kneeled, spraying the executioner with their blood, and Chang Tak Meng was killed as he lay on his back and sang. Yue Fat went with the soldiers to a dozen plundered villages, leaving a head at each and reading an Imperial proclamation which he had composed on the road.

He had done nothing to secure the victory, yet was touched as he read the assertions about justice and the Imperial writ. Even his own three soldiers, so derided by secretary Chang, were purposeful among their comrades and were rewarded with bullets and bags of powder, spending the winter in target practice with the sergeant's musket, their only gun, chipping white scars on the midstream rocks, angering the fisher folk.

Yue was relaxing after his adventure, considering this new role and drafting a request for a larger garrison, when the troublemaker Chang arrived with his strange confidence and his glib familiarity with the names of senior officials. Then came the two missionaries, so that Yue's life became neither action nor contemplation but instead the handling of people, who are complicated and boring. And now the white man stood in his doorway.

'I'm glad to see you,' said Yue Fat nervously. 'You will be concerned about your wife. She has gone into the mountains, wishing to meet the mountain people. She will soon return, I think. I hope you are well. We were surprised when you left us. I regret that I cannot offer you a proper hospitality, having been a victim of thieves, who were drunk.'

John sat down without invitation. He lay back in the chair, letting his tiredness rise up for a moment. He said, 'Your soldiers tried to kill me. Now you must give me money.'

There was no answer, and the collector flinched as John leapt up. He began to search the house, Yue Fat trailing behind. It didn't take long, because the house was so similar to his own. Even by lamplight he could see the loose brick in the oven.

There was a remarkable amount. In a steel box were loops of copper coins, their central holes threaded on grubby string, and below them were silver ingots from the Yi opium growers. John took the box and went back down the slope, the yelps of Yue Fat fading behind him.

He stood on the beach in the moonlight. The spring floods had grown and the black river reached almost to the stilts of the fisher folk houses. The water was so quiet in the shallows that even stars were reflected, though sometimes they were tadpoles of light that squirmed in the wavelets. Perhaps Yue Fat was right, and he should wait here for Grace.

Someone was walking across the beach. 'You must rest,' whispered one of the aunts.

'Where is my wife?' said John.

'She went upstream. She went with Jivu Lanu and the boy-loving secretary.' The aunt laughed softly and John saw that she was drunk. 'Come to my house.'

He said, 'Little Niece is drowned. Shen is dead.' He looked again over the black river. It reached to his feet, shiny as a ballroom floor, though only Little Niece could venture there.

'Your wife is mad, like the headman,' said the aunt. 'It's your fault, because you are too handsome, too handsome.' She laid a hand on his arm, hard like the hand of Little Niece.

John gave her the collector's box, keeping only a string of coins. He walked for an hour along the tribal path beside the river, then climbed the wooded valley side and gathered a bed of pine needles as the moon rose. When he woke, sunlight had slid into the valley, though there were parts it would never reach. He looked at the sky to check the shadow on his vision, but it fled from his gaze.

Perhaps Grace had left a letter. Perhaps it had been lost when their house was raided, or she had given it to Yue Fat, who would need only a friendly word to reveal it.

He got up with creaking muscles and continued upstream. It was best to leave the pebble beach and the cunning talk. He remembered how Yue Fat's scroll of the river had been spilled across the room by the fisher folk who robbed him. John wished he had taken the scroll: not all of it, only the part which showed the white spaces above the river. He walked into the wind which flowed from the mountains. It was clean and cold, having crossed the Himalayas unstained by voices.

Jivu Lanu had never before paid for shelter. But he had Chang's money, and today had searched Grace's bag with insolent calm while they rested on a high path. He was inclined to extravagance, and chose a Muslim inn. These charged four times more than Chinese houses because they were noted for fighting off bandits.

He booked only one room, but she despaired of an appeal to the landlord, who smoked, drank the horrible wine, and wore his blue turban only when in the court-yard drying horse dung for fuel: indoors he used it to hold up his trousers. His daughter also showed none of the restraints of Islam, pushing a finger through the paper windows of their room, her curiosity about the foreign demon accompanied by inviting smiles for Jivu.

'Three Muslims is one Muslim, two Muslims is half a Muslim, and one Muslim is no Muslim,' said Jivu, nodding wisely. He rolled back on his mat, complacently viewing their room by the light of a wick floating in a chipped teacup of stinking black oil.

From his pack he took cotton thread infused with chewed tea leaves and mercury, explaining how lice took the bait, swelled up, turned red and died. He came to tie the thread around her waist, but her anger was prompt and he sat back defeated.

They lay awake for hours on their separate mats.

21

They had left the inn at Jivu Lanu's insistence, as if it was a scene of humiliation, and now slept at one of his regular stops, a poor village in a rocky valley. *As usual in China the birds are absent*, Grace wrote, *destroyed even here by the hunger of Man, who has wrecked the gallery of beauty which the Creator placed on Earth for our delight and sustenance.*

They stayed with a woman and her daughter in a stone hut thatched with grass. Its one room was divided by a wicker screen: behind it was an inner chamber where the animals slept. Each morning, in a cloud of insects, a cow and a goat passed through the living quarters on their way to pasture. At night Grace laid her head on a wooden pillow against the screen, through which the goat pushed his snout and sniffed the stranger.

She remembered the Western pillows she had bought for their marriage bed, though John felt suffocated on the dusty bags, and felt his head roll and thought that his neck might break as he slept. She groaned with shame, recalling how she had forbidden Mandarin or Cantonese at home, even when John forgot the English word. And she had pestered him out of his Cantonese table manners – though this was impossible to regret.

Jivu made no further attempt on her person, instead

sitting with other households in day-long conversations about the flight of birds, the flow of blood, and how the body grows exhausted and requires a tonic: here he would open his pack. At morning and evening, though, he smirked at Grace as if marking another day of her captivity.

She sat on a padded stone, watching the wood fire in its pit. She wrote: *Even while cooking, the Chinese peasant betrays his poverty, the food being seared swiftly in a pan, in contrast to the baking and simmering of Western cuisine.* Flies blundered around the room or dropped on her journal like spent bullets. She added: *I am at present travelling in the hills. It is most interesting.*

Indeed, it was best to be away from the mission and her humiliation and to ease her sorrow with useful work. She wrote: *I will go perhaps even as far as the high country of the Yi, whom the Chinese call the 'Lolo', this being an insulting onomatopoeia referring to their inability to speak a Chinese language, a derivation identical to our words 'Tartar' and 'barbarian'.*

In her hesitant Mandarin she talked of Jesus with the girl, who was perhaps twelve years old and stood wide-eyed and scratching, staring at the foreigner's shoes, which were made of black sections like a beetle. Jivu smiled again, and Grace said, 'You confuse my truth with your lies.'

Jivu said, 'I once went to the source of the river. I will tell you about this journey. I went only once, because it is a very difficult journey, in which a man must cross the tiger country. Here the king is a tiger on a golden throne and the tigers fight in armies like wolves. I wore a cloak of clouds and wasn't seen, and climbed higher than birds and found the source of the river. Downstream there are silly fisher folk, known to me and to this honourable lady, and they believe that the river comes from the sky. They think it flows from the high heaven, then crosses the sky as the Milky Way, then pours into the mountains, then flows across the lands of men, then enters the sea at Hong Kong, then goes down to the world of ghosts. They are silly and ignorant. The source of the river is no more than an ordinary spring in a hillside, and its stream is thinner than a hair of your head. In fact it is so small that I plugged the spring with my little finger – this little finger, on my left hand, which is very small – and I made the whole river dry up, all the way to the sea, and only unstopped it for the poor fish and for the silly fisher folk who depend on them. That is the story of my journey to the source of the river.'

Grace wrote: *What is the purpose of these stories, so clearly false, except as an insult?* But next day the girl said to Jivu, 'Will you take me to the tiger country? I want to see you stop the waters of the river.'

Jivu wasn't interested in a dirty peasant girl, no matter how young. He wanted the half-white woman, who was clean and rich with an important black book. He thought he understood Chinese characters, which were somehow drawings of a face when it said each sound, but the barbarian words were more cunning. He didn't wish to learn from the woman, however: instead she would see his own great powers.

John climbed all morning, the way then levelling to traverse a sodden forest. Around noon he slithered on pine needles down a wooded gully, harassed by biting flies in the still air, until the trees fell back. The path now crossed a flat headland enclosed by a bend in the river, and he trudged uphill through rough meadows, his head very painful. He hardly noticed the porters on the path, but drew close to their barrow, whose squeak would drive away demons.

The road was also propitious. Alone John would not have followed its zigzags: but a straight road aims at your back like a rifle. Dizzy and sick, he followed the porters round the unnecessary bends, which would throw off a rushing demon, and sat with them when they rested, because demons come to a solitary man. Stones lay about for seats, but the porters sat on the ground and used the stones for their packs, which would therefore be easier to lift. They gave him *tsamba*, a dust of barley and red beans, and he was cheered because he had never eaten this famously disgusting staple.

Later, as he followed the barrow along the edge of a pine forest, he wondered if the shadow in his vision was the ghost of his old amah, Song Lan. Would she guide him to his wife, who she had once resented?

Grace was wearied by a constant flute music. The young men of the village practised as if for a festival, and the buzzing drone was like the bagpipes of Scottish regiments on gala days in Hong Kong.

But one night the music came from beyond the village. The young men stood in the darkness, their music blurred in the warm night. Grace shivered at their soft laughter and the gentle persuasions of the flutes.

In a moment the daughter of the house was gone. She was a breastless child, but joined the girls in the village yard, seizing their hands and taking her place in the firelight. Now they were dancing, bent by the music into a stiff posture which slowly transformed to another such stillness. Perhaps the postures spelt out a meaning, thought Grace, but they seemed no more than delicious cramps, like your first stretch in the morning.

The boys moved closer, their laughter stilled, all their thought in the soft music, which became more mellow, richer, more inventive. Grace could see why the girls moved from solemnity to short laughs of joy.

Now couples moved into the dark, or into the Village House, which was decorated with fresh blooms. At last the child from her house seized a partner, and drew him into the night. Grace looked at the child's mother, whose eyes were misted with the melancholy of any parent at any coming-of-age.

When had the porters changed? The wheelbarrow had gone, and John heard the familiar mutterings of 'Kill, kill,' though now in Mandarin. The new porters were bent under ugly wooden frames, and turned their necks like turtles to frown at him. He asked them about Grace,

Jivu Lanu and secretary Chang, but they cursed and spat.

He had grown up with hatred, the Cantonese drawing a finger over their throats as he passed. But now he was sunk under the weight of his wound and the porters were very oppressive. His recourse was a flood of coolness which perhaps came from the Buddha.

He drifted to the tail of the procession, walking silently beside a boy monk until they came to a resting place. John sat down carefully on a rock. The boy laughed, then demanded alms. Speaking slowly around the pain in his head, John asked his questions.

'Jivu Lanu?' said the boy. 'Who doesn't know him!'

'You're sure? Jivu Lanu the shaman?'

'He's a friend of our lama,' said the boy. 'He trades a little opium, and brings news from the high valleys, where the disgusting Chinese are spreading.'

'Your monastery,' said John, 'are you going there now?' But the boy was begging among the porters.

Now they traversed steep slopes through close-set pine woods, stepping over bustling streams, the green river glimmering below them through the trees, until they reached a nest of ragged flags at the mouth of a side valley, John always watching the boy monk. The porters passed on, teetering across the tributary stream on slick rocks, while the youngster bowed, having fared well at his begging.

John stared at the prayer flags, wedged among rocks and giving tongue to the wind, and felt weak before these banners of the Buddha. But the boy was scrambling up the side valley and he had to follow, though the track pulsed with his hurt.

He passed an old cairn and climbed beside the boisterous stream through a landscape of stones. The boy had disappeared, but ahead was the monastery, a ramshackle place, its roofs sunken and weeds in the walls. He eyed it like a fort, however, because God ruled the light and demons ruled the dark but the Buddha's silence surrounded it all.

He was not observed, and the main gate was open and unguarded. Inside was a square courtyard full of weeds, where an old monk filled a bucket at a walled pool. He stared at John in amazement, then hurried to the main building.

No one came so John went inside. There was a large hall, very smoky, with bare beams across the ceiling and a dozen monks sitting idle. He sat against the wall on a long bench. Its only covering was a thin cloth, but he sat in silence until evening, when a monk brought him bean curds, rice, greens, tea and water. The room grew cold and the outside doors were barred.

The room emptied and all was quiet except for the slippers of the younger monks as they patrolled. He shivered in the mountain chill and woke several times in the night. Once a watchman cried, 'It is the second watch. Be still. Banish improper thoughts and with all your hearts think of the Buddha.'

John wanted to stay on the bench, but someone was pulling his sleeve. It was the boy monk, who laughed and wouldn't leave. 'I'm ill,' said John, delighting the boy, who drew him through cold corridors and up stone steps to the tongueless temple bells. 'My duty is to strike them with hammers,' said the boy, sniggering. 'I have not done so since the last New Year.'

'Let me rest.'

'Yes. I will take you to the dormitory.' But the boy was lying and hurried on, his bare soles smacking the stone floor and John hopping on his heels down steps made for Oriental feet. The boy howled like a dog at each door 'to give the Buddha notice of a barbarian' and brought him to the holy of holies where a relic of the Buddha – precisely what could not be revealed – was hidden behind carved screens under a tinselled pagoda taller than a man.

'This room was our library,' said the urchin. 'But Lao Tze said, "The Way that can be discussed is not the true Way." We sold the books and instead bought this relic. If an infidel such as you were to touch it, there would be an explosion like an earthquake.'

'Why did you become a monk?' said John.

'Poverty and nothing else.'

They went out through a side door above the stream. John groaned as the boy pulled him down the steep bank, across the stream on rough boulders, then up the far side among a score of small brick domes, each with a window the size of a hand with neither glass nor paper to keep out the cold.

Many of the monks had seemed near idiots, but John had blamed Buddhism and their empty lives. Now, as they approached a brick dome, he saw a billow of smoke from its window. The boy snatched open the low door. The monk was far gone in his habit, speechless as the Buddha, a bamboo pipe in his lap.

'You see?' said the boy. 'This is good opium.' He laughed and wiped his nose on his smock. 'I will make a pipe for you. You have money?'

He was astonished at John's refusal, then angry: wasn't opium also called 'European mud'? John's head was bowed with pain, so he watched through his eyebrows as the boy scrambled cursing back to the monastery.

That night he curled in a dormitory where the monks lay in their day clothes on thin mats. Finally he saw books. There was a Buddhist tract with woodcuts of the Enlightened One, but most were street literature, gross and obscene: sniggering, a monk showed him a stereoscope and its pornographic plates.

He woke at dawn, too cold to sleep. The monks still snored, but he put on his cold sandals and wandered the corridors. He opened the side door and watched rain slanting through the narrow valley. Rocks lay about, slick with water: on one, a crow disputed with the wind. The shadow in his sight seemed bigger and darker against the veils of rain.

He had been swept from the pebble beach on a fresh but dry morning. In his linen shirt and trousers he stared along the way he would have to go – down the valley slope, across the stream, and up past wet boulders into the driving rain. He was linked to a woman by promises made in Canton, but the cold wind could blow them away.

He felt the dislocation of the Buddha but fought it off. Nevertheless he turned back into the monastery. It would be foolish to go out in the rain. To become ill would only impede his mission.

Grace was struggling up another slope but staring towards the high mountains, beyond which lay Tibet, then India, and at last the Holy Land. Perhaps she was stepping on the very path that the sons of Noah had used as they came into China from the far west beyond the sunset.

She thought of the character for west, 西, and at once saw that it was made of the familiar characters for first, 一, and man, 儿, but this time combined with 囗, which meant enclosure but again might easily mean garden.

She fell to her knees. She gripped her hands together, because she had been granted a revelation. The Lord had shown her how the descendants of Adam recalled the primal garden as they looked westward, as she did now, from the lands of the east!

She would save China for Christ. She would work and work. She would be alone but filled with zeal, bringing the Chinese to the Lord, doubling Christendom. Gathered to the Kingdom, China would welcome Western thought: medicine would end its plagues; democracy would topple its tyrants; factories would bring prosperity; knowledge would speed on iron rails to the heart of the nation.

She saw a little church among rice fields, where tiny

figures stooped. One of them straightened for a moment, as people do in a rice field, and glanced across to the village and saw the brave cross on the steeple.

Only a Christian and a Chinese could have found these messages among the characters. Kneeling, she prayed to be released from these mountains so that she could bring her knowledge to the world. She gave thanks for her mixed blood, which was holy, and ignored the curses of Jivu Lanu.

John had bought a cape from one of the monks, so the cold no longer disturbed him. He couldn't lie on his right side, but otherwise dozed quietly in the dormitory, wondering if Jivu Lanu would come: if not, how could he be found? The pain sang in his ear and half-closed his eye, so he followed the Buddha into silence.

The boy monk came. He pulled down John's blanket, sitting back to watch as the white giant groaned and stirred. He uncovered the huge feet and laughed with the other monks. He twisted the toes, sticky and white as rice balls, until the giant roused himself and could be led to the great hall.

John swayed in front of the fire. A stranger in Tartar dress watched from the best chair, then stood, the better to exhibit his pride: he struck his breast and declared, in a great blast of garlic, that his name was Ku Ch'ingtze. He sat down and stretched his legs, smiling at the white man who was large but weak. 'I've known many of your people,' he said. 'I was a trader around the river mouth where the white barbarians live.'

John, speaking as if drunk, said, 'Yes, I come from there.'

Ku Ch'ingtze said again, 'I was a trader,' so that John thought, 'A pirate.'

Ku stared at John and laughed, because the white man was helpless. 'What do you think of this monastery? Isn't it comfortable? In my youth I was a novice here, like this poor urchin. I was beaten every day till I escaped downriver. The fault lay with the old lama, who made the monks rise early and stopped them trading opium.

'Now I live by slave-trading and fighting. At present I'm looking for escaped slaves to return to the Yi in the Cool Mountains, where they'll be killed or hamstrung at the ankles.' He said this with amusement, staring at the monks in case they challenged his right to carry them away.

The boy monk had been pulling at John's sleeve. Finally the youngster said: 'Ku Ch'ingtze, Ku Ch'ingtze, tell the white man about Jivu Lanu, your friend!'

Ku narrowed his eyes. 'Who would want to know this thing, and why?'

'I'm a traveller like yourself,' said John. 'I know Jivu Lanu from the lowlands, where he stayed with another friend called Yue Fat, a tax collector. I'm looking for a guide into the mountains and Jivu Lanu would be suitable.'

'A guide!' said Ku. 'I'll be your guide. Who knows these mountains better than I? And who can better protect you than one whose waistcoat – even in summer – is a double thickness of sheepskin, proof against any blade, and whose right arm is bare in the coldest winter, ready for swordplay?'

'Yes. That would be useful. But still I want to find Jivu Lanu. We have business to arrange, and he has some money of mine.'

Ku Ch'ingtze frowned with impressive thought. 'Ask these men,' he said, gesturing to the monks. 'In the old days things were hard: now they are comfortable. This improvement is thanks to me, because I removed the old lama. I did this for revenge, but also because the old man was starting a second monastery to the north, giving away our wealth and bringing hardship and work. I discussed this with the under-lama: on a journey to survey the new site, we pushed the lama into the river.'

The lama had not been seen for a year, said Ku, but had then returned to the monastery demanding his old position. But the under-lama, with access to the monastery's wealth, had easily retained his power. 'We drove the old lama into the hills, where perhaps he has found enlightenment, and the monastery has again become what it should be, a place where the monks seek wisdom without the distractions of cold and hunger. This is thanks to me.'

John was too dizzy to speak, so Ku laughed again. 'You are wise to select me. For one so young, Jivu Lanu is already dangerous.' He drew his great Russian cutlass with caressing smoothness, and turned it to catch the light, explaining that no sooner had the old lama been expelled than the new one had to kill his own brother, whose greed had become irritating.

On the advice of Ku Ch'ingtze, the lama had paid a Boxer 200 dollars to carry out the killing, and the brother had been ambushed on a mountain path. The lama had watched the murder for fear that the Boxer would steal something and implicate them, but the brother was killed without difficulty and thrown with his possessions down the cliff.

Two days later the Boxer had come to the dead man's funeral to collect his payment, but was instead sacrificed at the graveside to appease the brother's ghost. 'A plan which I myself suggested,' said Ku, stropping his cutlass on the tops of his boots. 'I would not do the murder, which seemed to me a dirty business. But Jivu Lanu was involved, so you see he is a villain.'

He pursed his lips. 'I'll be your guide. It's agreed. With me you'll soon find Jivu Lanu. We'll begin tomorrow. Can you be ready?' He took a clove of garlic from a wooden plate on the floor and crunched it like a cherry, washing it down with Chinese brandy.

John wanted only to sleep, but Ku Ch'ingtze stood and gripped his shoulder. 'You are the first man I've seen who is taller than me.'

22

Grace and Jivu Lanu were in a cheap inn, forced there by rain and sharing a single room with shepherds and porters, much troubled by smells and vermin. The single character 天, meaning 'heaven', was daubed on the wall in red paint.

There was one lamp, which she set beside her, though its dirty peanut oil dropped smuts on her Bible. She was weary and read again how Paul had suffered for the Gospel: 'five times received I forty stripes save one. Thrice was I beaten with rods, once was I stoned, thrice I suffered shipwreck'.

She wondered how many had dipped a finger in their tears to turn to Deuteronomy, where it is promised that the good man 'shall be like a tree planted by the rivers of water ... and whatsoever he doeth shall prosper. The ungodly are not so: but are like chaff which the wind driveth away.'

But she was too good a scholar for such reassurance: God had denied that men could understand His ways, and demanded of Job, 'Where wast thou when I laid the foundations of the earth? Have the gates of death been opened unto thee? Hast thou given the horse strength? Doth the eagle mount up at thy command, and make her nest on high?'

She and John had known the same desolation: a parent dead, the other unfeeling. She had thought that marriage and the Lord's service would redress it all, but John had vanished down the river.

And he had been right to go. He had broken his word, as a healthy animal breaks its tether. She didn't belong in such happiness, and thought in wonder of her marriage, which was vanity and folly.

She stared into the lamp, wondering how to escape Jivu Lanu.

John followed Ku Ch'ingtze from the side door of the monastery and into bright sunshine. They crossed the stream and climbed the valley side, passing the brick contemplation cells and turning upstream, while pain thumped in the roots of his teeth.

They tracked above the stream, skirting fallen boulders, slithering on shale, the water spurting below, until they came to the head of the valley where a waterfall spouted from a cliff. They climbed beside the falls to a notch in the cliff face, then into a narrow gully cut by the stream. John touched a sticky discharge on the back of his head.

They clambered over fallen slabs of rock, which choked the gully like coins in a purse, the water burrowing under them as naked as miners, or slapping its hands about, or rolling like lovers among whispers and sniggers. His ears were troubled with slobberings of the pig trough, digestive gurglings, echoing trickles of the urinal.

The gully dwindled to a dead end full of ferns, where

they climbed a stair of wet rubble to an upland meadow. They crossed a dome of turf and bare rock and descended a broad grassland with stands of bamboo, then came back to the river, or perhaps a tributary of the river, and took a narrow path along the side of a steepening scarp.

'This path is famous,' said Ku. 'It's called the Waistband of the Fat Mandarin.'

They were crossing the belly of a rounded cliff, the path as narrow as their shoes. Far below, the river stampeded through an echoing gorge, the spray rising like dust. A warm wind blew their hair forward as they balanced across the bare rock, steep as a roof, with nothing to hold and China spinning around them.

'A family came along this path,' said Ku, shouting over his shoulder. 'There was a mother, a father, three children, and a kitten on a string, which the smallest daughter was carrying. The kitten leapt at a butterfly and fell down the cliff.

'The daughter was a clever child and dropped the string, but watched the kitten fall and therefore followed it down. The next daughter, watching her sister, toppled after her. The mother followed. She was holding their only son and so drew the father. The butterfly drifted away on the breeze.

'This was a favourite story of the old lama, and shows the danger of possessions.'

The cliff face grew steeper until it jostled their elbows, then bumped their shoulders. John now embraced the rock, shuffling sideways, his eyes closed, feeling with his feet, the path swaying like a tightrope. But the steepening cliff was pushing him over the drop, so that he hugged it desperately. He opened his eyes and found that the cliff had fallen back and he was leaning against it, pushing against his own weight while Ku laughed.

They were at the apex of the pot-bellied cliff. John's knees were shaking so they sat against the slope, their heels wedged in the path. He touched the bulging face of the cliff, larger than the Great Buddha at Leshan, and saw how the rock was layered like pages, the path running where a softer layer had worn away. He thought of rain scouring the cliff while God was busy elsewhere.

Grace and the shaman were climbing through a sloping meadow full of flowers. It was a beautiful morning, warm in the sunshine but the air cold, as they climbed beside a little stream, nameless as an orphan, which glittered in the sun. Jivu Lanu had declared that the mountains were now dangerous and they must be roped together. But the rope was only a leather thong, held loosely by Jivu Lanu and tied to her wrist in greasy knots.

She thought of the character for west and fretted that she was trapped in these tongueless hills and couldn't reveal her news to the world. She sang 'Guide me, O thou Great Jehovah', 'Oh, happy day', 'Rock of Ages' and 'O God Our Help in Ages Past'.

They met a group of Miao hunters, and Grace called for help, but her Mandarin proved impenetrable. 'She is possessed by a red-haired demon,' said Jivu, and pulled the leather thong.

Grace remembered 2 Kings 9:35: 'they found no more of her than the skull, and the feet, and the palms of her hands'; and 2 Samuel 14:14, which says, 'For we needs must die, and are as water spilt on the ground, which cannot be gathered up again; neither doth God respect any person'; and 1 Chronicles 29:15, which says that we are 'sojourners, as were all our fathers: our days on the earth are as a shadow, and there is none abiding'.

She looked at Jivu Lanu as a woman looks at a new suitor. There were now two men in her life – one she had married, and one who contemplated her death.

On the side of a rocky valley, among thorn trees and low scrub, John and Ku Ch'ingtze walked through crops scratched in the thin earth. A dozen women ran away, but an old man, too dignified to flee, tended a smudge of fire among the scrub. He was obliged to lead them to the village.

It was very pretty. Children watched gravely from the branches of trees, which leant over the houses like parents. They were given water. Ku stood in careless pride in the village yard while John asked about Grace, Jivu Lanu, and the little secretary – at which the villagers grew solemn.

They were taken to a field behind the huts. John's heart almost failed him, because a pile of stones lay on an obvious grave. He dug in a frenzy, but was held back. He stood against a hut, watching the work.

It was secretary Chang. 'We thought he had gone

home,' said the old man. 'The shaman said so. A few days later we found him. He was bitten by animals, as you see.'

But no animal had killed him, thought John. The old man, chuckling nervously, pointed to the great gash on Chang's belly and explained its purpose – it was designed so that a knee in the belly would force out the liver, so that the *qi* might be eaten.

The dusty lips of the gash ran down the breastbone, then forked into two. It made the striding shape 人, which is the Chinese character for 'man'.

They had come to the river again and Grace paddled briefly in the icy water. She sat on a rock, rubbing her Chinese feet, though Jivu Lanu jerked at the leather cord around her wrist. Bound feet were the opposite of a peasant's flat feet, she thought: was this their attraction?

She looked at her square hands, then touched her hair, stiff as wire. She was like a peasant woman, she thought, dragged through the hills behind her man.

Jivu pulled her from the rock, and in her anger she remembered the women at the Mission House in Hong Kong and how they had sighed at China's wickedness. Indeed, this wickedness was now more surprising, because Grace had proved that the Chinese had once known the Lord.

She stopped in amazement. She had been struck by a great insight. Jivu Lanu hauled on the cord, which was most painful, but she was too astonished to move.

She had been wrong about the Chinese, and so had

every missionary, and so had all of Christendom. The Chinese were not benighted heathens, to be pitied for their ignorance. Instead they were the Lord's betrayers.

The Chinese had once known God: her discoveries among Chinese characters had proved that. Yet now they worshipped idols. It followed that they had broken the first two commandments, the dread prohibitions revealed to Moses on Mount Sinai while the Israelites bowed to their idols in the valley below: 'Thou shalt have no other gods before me. Thou shalt not make unto thee any graven image, or any likeness of anything that is in heaven above, or that is in the earth beneath, or that is in the water under the earth. Thou shalt not bow down thyself to them, nor serve them: for I the Lord thy God am a jealous God.'

In a fury of excitement, ignoring the shouts of Jivu Lanu, she turned to Exodus, reading aloud the half-remembered curse as the leather thong jerked her wrist: 'for I the Lord thy God am a jealous God, visiting the iniquity of the fathers upon the children unto the third and fourth generation of them that hate me'.

She stood in amazement. Indeed the Lord's anger had endured – so that millions were killed in inexplicable wars, in restless rivers, in plague and earthquake, until the living couldn't bury the dead. Ignorance and cruelty through China's generations, even to a helpless missionary in the hills.

She was possessed by this vision of China, confirmed in wickedness, its people rending each other like creatures of the deep, destroying all who would help them. She had blamed her husband, but he too was drowned in its wickedness. She pulled back on the leather thong, raising her fists to Jivu Lanu, shouting, 'Chinese! You are Chinese!'

He snatched her Bible and threw it into the river. They struggled over her journal, Grace aiming her nails at his eyes, then it too was floating away.

Jivu Lanu punched her.

John kept leaping up to save his wife. Ku Ch'ingtze led him from the grave of secretary Chang and gave him a twist of paper. It was a medicine, he said, made by the lama and a tonic for those exhausted in the hills.

John opened the paper, which was empty. But Ku pointed to scrawled writing in the lama's hand, which was as good as medicine: moreover the paper was sealed with the lama's spit.

As John chewed the paper, the villagers pointed to the trail that Jivu Lanu and the half-white woman had taken. Jivu was maintaining his route to his home village and would be funnelled into the high passes, where he could be caught.

There were no able-bodied men in the village to stop John taking bags of barley and maize meal. He threw down some of Yue Fat's money, but had to brush aside the women who shrieked and held up their babies. As they climbed the path into a cold wind he thought, 'We should have taken blankets.'

23

Nothing in the sergeant's career had been so hard as coming back to the pebble beach. After John had leapt off the great raft, the two soldiers had tried to hire its rowing boat. But the crew, exhausted by their struggle with the sea anchor, refused every bribe to search for the white man and the young soldier.

By the time the rowing boat was ready the river had changed again: black mudflats lay against the banks, thick with wind-borne weeds which had sprouted through the winter. Again the soldiers had to leap into muddy shallows, splashing to the bank as the rowing boat hurried away.

Against the advice of the raft men they turned upstream, at once coming to a tributary where they trekked inland to find a crossing point. They hiked all day on an animal track through bamboo woods as dense as fur and tall as towers, then lay in a haze of mosquitoes which their smokiest campfire couldn't disperse. Next day they stared at the island where the long-nose might be hiding, but could do nothing, and at dusk they reached the town where he had found a boat.

But the captains only bowed and said they did not take passengers, 'especially honoured Imperial soldiers such as you, who deserve the best of accommodation'.

Secretly the captains thought how soldiers never paid for their passage and were sometimes curious about packages hidden under the bilge boards. The soldiers finally offered sufficient payment, then fretted over the boat's slow pace, and at last like John were driven ashore by the wearisome rapids.

Then the corporal became difficult. He was thirty-five, an age when soldiers are miserable. For months he had performed his duties slowly because they interrupted his brooding, and he had abandoned alcohol because it muddled his thoughts of how he had given his youth to the service and had no home or children and only the prospect of hopeless wandering in the world of ghosts. And now the track was steep and rocky along the river-bank and carried him to the lonely uplands.

He would lag far behind, half hidden under his torn umbrella, his spear trailing, while the sergeant sat by the path and waited. When the corporal arrived, one or other would say, 'We must be faithful to Yue Fat,' though this had ceased to be funny.

It was midmorning when they came to the beach of the fisher folk, yet no one was working. The headman stared at them from under his house, and the aunts rose in alarm from their seats around the fire. The two soldiers hitched their packs and climbed the slope to the collector's house, creeping silently into their hut, hoping to rest.

But at once the collector appeared. He stood in their doorway while the sergeant described how they had found the two fugitives, how Little Niece had jumped into the river and disappeared, how the white barbarian had been shot in the head and killed, and how the foolish young private had drowned as he tried to retrieve the body.

'The white man was here, you fool,' screamed Yue Fat. 'He attacked me and stole the tax money. Go at once. Return with his head.' Yue said nothing about the raid by the aunts, which was too humiliating.

Stunned, the soldiers sat on their bunks, then ate, then gathered their kit. They started upriver at noon, angry with their life and each other, and for two days the corporal said only, 'We won't catch this white monster.'

The sergeant secretly agreed. When they came to the monastery he decided they would stay for a few days, then return to Yue Fat claiming that the white man was lost. But instead they met the boy monk.

He danced around them. He drew them down a corridor, running backwards, laughing, wiping his nose on the front of his smock and boasting how he had brought the white barbarian to the monastery and had introduced him to that great man Ku Ch'ingtze, of whom the soldiers had doubtless heard. He threw open a side door and leant into the mist, pointing to the path across the stream which Ku Ch'ingtze and the white man were taking to Jivu Lanu's home village. He took the sergeant's arm. 'Do the honoured guests require a pipe?' he said.

The two soldiers sat in the great hall while monks bowed and brought food. The sergeant said, 'This monastery is a great resort of travellers on the river. We should wait here for the white man.' But the corporal looked at him with a crooked smile and the sergeant thought, 'Disobedience is a disease that can spread.'

Next morning they travelled on, toiling up past the waterfall and through the gully choked with boulders and across the round belly of the riverside cliff, the corporal incredulous and saying, 'Your honour, why do we do this?'

The boy monk's directions had been very clear, but still the sergeant was surprised when they found the white man and his companion.

Ku Ch'ingtze hated the land. His knees and ankles pined for the pirate ship where he had spent his glory days, the deck tipping under his bare feet, the shiver through the keel as they crossed the line between river and sea in the waters near Hong Kong.

Then British guns sank them, so he had run a rat farm in a pirate village across the estuary because the stupid whites were cleaning Hong Kong and paid 20 cents for rat tails. He was ashamed, and when the barbarians burned the village he smuggled opium through the muddy channels round Canton, though he felt clumsy on the little boats and too large among their petty grinning crews. He argued with their captains, who were nothing compared to his former chief, torn in half by barbarian grapeshot, and with each dispute he moved upstream.

In the riverside towns his height was embarrassing, and his great brass-bound scabbard snagged in the gangways of the little boats, where you were either a captain or a coolie. He pitched one captain into the river, planning to seize his boat, but saw how the crew was waiting for him to sleep, and again wandered towards his old home in the hills.

One day, far upriver, he was stacking pigs in baskets six deep across the deck, the lower ones crushed and shrieking, the upper ones voiding on his clothes. He had done nothing illegal for a month, except to take a handful of dried sweet potato from a peasant woman. He said, 'This boat is smaller than my shoe, so I might as well walk,' and stepped for good on to the shameful land, where you must carry everything.

Only the mountains were a consolation: their solitude flattered his pride. But still he felt encumbered. When he faced down a rival, or delivered a slave to the Yi, it was with defiance, as if in the face of criticism. He seemed to say, 'You were wrong: I am still important, though now on land.'

He had begun to pluck grey hairs from his beard, and no longer hungered for the next valley. He spent ever longer at the monastery, and dreamt of some kindly woman with a garden; he knew of two candidates, and another whose husband could be driven away.

His bad temper often found an outlet, and he had come to resent the white giant, who was a cousin to the men who had driven him from Hong Kong, and was making him walk quickly. He had planned to rob him, either alone or with Jivu Lanu, but this hike through the hills was cooling his ardour. At last he sat heavily in a wooded gully above the river and demanded to rest. He was lighting his second pipeful when the two soldiers appeared.

He eyed them without appetite: the younger soldier looked too miserable to fight, but the shrivelled old man had climbed a few paces off the trail and now leant against a tree, watching them over the smoking fuse of his musket. All three had slyly loosened their swords and knew that the others had done likewise.

A discussion followed, which Ku ignored: he didn't care why the soldiers wanted the white man, only reckoning the value of their armour and weapons. Finally the talk descended to short words and longer pauses. Ku noted with approval that cautious glances were cast his way. Now it would start.

The corporal laid a hand on the barbarian's arm, but was brushed aside. The sergeant said, 'No, no,' meaning that such a fuss was unworthy. The barbarian stood firm, and the sergeant smiled at Ku as if to say, 'How foolish are these foreigners.' Finally, with a nod from the sergeant, the corporal levelled his spear. Now only fighting could result, and John remembered his religion.

He said, 'Ku Ch'ingtze, we must not harm these men.'

'Indeed,' said the sergeant from his place above the trail. 'We won't fight over a barbarian, who has come to trouble the Empire.'

'I myself will chose when to fight,' said Ku.

'Certainly,' said the sergeant. 'But we must not hazard our lives for one like this, who spreads the barbarian religion. Unless you yourself worship the god with the red beard.'

'We won't fight, Ku Ch'ingtze,' said John, and at once the corporal searched him, taking Yue Fat's money.

Ku poked at the dust with the toe of his boot. He thought, 'After all, this is not my argument.' He noticed the money, however.

As they departed down the trail, the white man shouted, 'Ku Ch'ingtze, thank you. God be with you.'

'My wife has been taken into the mountains. She is a prisoner of Jivu Lanu, who murdered secretary Chang. I saw Chang's body. He had been cut open. We should capture Jivu and free my wife.'

But again the spear pricked his back, so John stumbled on. His thumbs were tied behind him, which was a remarkable impediment on these steep trails, but still he talked, pleading and persuading.

'Walk on, younger brother,' said the sergeant.

At dusk they camped in a narrow valley full of bushes, John renewing his pleas and the two soldiers sitting apart. The corporal whispered, 'But we are going back, honoured sir? We have had enough of the hills, surely.'

'We will follow orders,' said the sergeant.

The corporal gathered his courage again. 'Your honour,' he said. 'Honoured sir, if the collector hears that his secretary was murdered then he will send us back to these mountains.'

'He won't hear it from the white man,' said the sergeant. 'Tomorrow we take him to the river.'

The soldiers were too cautious to light a fire, but there was a little moonlight and they were sheltered from the mountain winds by the bushes and the steep slopes above. John's thumbs were still bound, and the corporal fed him *tsamba*. The corporal's eyes were suddenly naked, though the look was gone in a moment. Did it mean that they meant to kill him?

'Why did you let my comrade drown?' said the corporal.

'I saw that the spirits wanted him. So I was the same as you.'

'Do you still carry my bullet?' said the sergeant.

That night John lay awake and heard a rustling in the bushes. He couldn't believe that the soldiers didn't hear it, and wondered if they planned a trap. He stretched to his full length, hoping to identify himself to Ku Ch'ingtze. He sat up, because Ku was among them.

Ku slashed at one of the sleepers, but the other was up in a moment and lost in the bushes. Ku spun round, cutlass ready, watching the wall of darkness, but no one came.

With the point of his cutlass he uncovered the face of the man he had cut. It was the corporal, his half-open eyes glinting in the moonlight. This meant that the sergeant had escaped, which was unfortunate, although a sword lay by his empty bed.

Reluctantly Ku Ch'ingtze cut John's bonds and gave him the sword. 'Keep watch,' he said. He began searching the camp for loot. As he passed the corporal, he stabbed him again through the blanket.

The corporal sat up, then stood slowly like an old man. He tottered into the dark, but tripped over his intestines and lay silent among the undergrowth. John went to him, finding his wrist in the darkness, but the man was dead.

John saw how the dark and the bushes favoured an attacker. He shivered and said, 'We must leave.'

Ku muttered as he searched the camp, but at last accepted that John's money had vanished with the sergeant. Their swords still drawn, guarding their flanks, they tracked across the valley to a strong position among thorn bushes.

John sat with the sergeant's sword across his knees, watching Ku Ch'ingtze sort his loot. Ku lit a fire, too angry to be cautious: he had failed to kill the sergeant and now must stay in the highlands, beyond the reach of the Empire, and would be a prey to every bandit and warlord. He cast a final look at John, clearly wondering how easy he would be to rob, but instead hoisted the great bundle of the soldiers' gear and walked into the night with a curse.

John threw thorn twigs on to the fire, then lay down: when the flames died a little he slipped away between the boulders, hoping that the sound of his progress would seem like a last crackling of the thorns.

He ran in the dark, throwing the sergeant's sword into the bushes and following a dried-up stream until he was breathless. He lay under a bush to watch and listen. The night birds resumed their song, but there was no other sound. He caught himself dozing and so ran on through the dark, more quietly this time, repeating this process until daybreak. He slept for an hour or two and was woken by a beetle crossing his face.

He ate a little *tsamba*, realizing that the idea of the thorn twigs had come from Ecclesiastes, where it is written, 'As the crackling of thorns under a pot, so is the laughter of the fool.' He had also been thinking of *The Art of War*, where armies are told to alter the number of their fires, so that they seem stronger or else seem weakened by desertion.

He smiled in the dark and thought, 'My mind is a half-breed.'

At dawn the sergeant was sitting in the bushes next to the corporal's body. He was checking his musket. It had been inside his blanket as protection against the dew, and he had taken it when Ku Ch'ingtze burst into the camp. He might have shot the two giants from the dark slopes around the camp, but the fuse cord had been pulled from his musket as he ran through the bushes. He had considered replacing it with a scrap of cloth from his uniform: instead he had shivered in the dark and wondered about his loyalty to Yue Fat.

Now he dragged the corporal's body against a boulder, covering it with the biggest rocks he could move, so that only a bear or tiger could molest it. The flies were bewildered, then found an entrance.

He walked back to the river and at once saw a wet footprint on a riverside boulder. He sat on a rock and stared at the print of the great sandal, which pointed upstream. The giant was still heading to Jivu Lanu's home village, and should be easy to trap.

The sergeant thought how he had no food and no blanket and how good it would be to walk down and down until the air was warm. But it was too cold to sit for long. He started upstream, muttering, 'Just a little way, just a little way.'

The river was a milky blue-green, coiling among boulders. The narrow valley was bare rock, with a straight line of forest above the floodline. Tributary streams fell with a clatter down the steep valley sides, crossing a faint path, no more than a strip of smaller stones, which ran beside the river.

'I'm too stupid to make choices,' thought the sergeant, 'even the choice to go back.'

He climbed into winter, following the prints like the pads of a bear. There were gusts of wet snow, a thing which he remembered from his childhood in the northern provinces.

Towards noon he saw the white man. The sergeant crouched behind a boulder and loaded his musket, though the barbarian was out of range. As he watched, though, John left the river, climbing a tributary stream which emerged from a ravine full of rocks.

Now he could trap the giant. He stared up the steep valley side, hesitating, then set off, slithering on stones then pushing up through trees, climbing into flurries of snow, the cold air scraping his throat while he whispered, 'This is the last thing I do for the Empire.'

He was on the ridge above the tributary stream. He

hurried through pine trees, the clouds of his breath as big as himself, then peered into the ravine. He had passed the white man, who perhaps was weakened by his wound.

Encouraged, the sergeant scratched his flint. He hurried further along the ridge, swinging the fuse cord, making rings of smoke and wondering if the big-nosed barbarian might smell it. He peered again into the ravine and saw the white man further behind. He crept down over fallen rocks and crouched behind a boulder. The white giant was on the far side of the ravine, coming towards him.

The sergeant's hand stuck to the cold barrel. He had no experience of shooting in the mountains and tried to think whether cold would affect the burning of the powder: but he had practised often at the pebble beach, where the winters were almost as cold, and thought not.

He aimed across the ravine at the point where the white man would pass. It was an easy shot to the head, but if he missed there would be time to reload, and the next shot would be interesting but not difficult, providing the snow didn't sweep back. On this broken ground, any injury would mean that his quarry was doomed.

John was wondering when he would reach the white spaces above the river. Then he saw the sergeant. He looked for cover, but heard a shot. The lead slug slapped into the rock face above his head. He touched the flattened slug. He began to peel it from the rock and then ran.

He ran downhill because every musket-man fears his bullet falling out, then continued upstream. He thought how Imperial matchlocks had a short grip like a pistol, which was held against the hip or chest to fire: but the sergeant had aimed like a Westerner, the grip at his cheek, snug and purposeful.

Now, thought John, the sergeant would be running behind him, well back so that he couldn't be attacked before he reloaded. He would take another bamboo container from his belt. As he ran he would tear off its paper cap and pour the powder into his musket, cursing because he had no time to clear the barrel of embers: every musket-man was tattooed with powder which had pre-ignited. Would the sergeant throw away the powder flask or replace it in his belt? Now he would drop the cylindrical slug down the barrel. Imperial matchlocks had no rammer and no wadding, so he would rap the butt on the track to settle the charge. Now he would crouch to aim.

The sergeant fired. Incredulous, he saw the bullet again hit the rock face over the white man's head. 'Shit on your ancestors,' he said. He ran on, bewildered. He kept the white giant in sight and reloaded. He dropped down to the bottom of the ravine and splashed through shallows where the going was easier.

They ran on under the iron sky. There was frost on the riverbank and a frill of ice around rocks in the shallows. They ran so long that the sergeant's musket cooled, splashes of river water freezing to the barrel. The snow swept back, but he kept the white man in view. A blast of cold air blew the snow away, leaving pellets of ice on his lacquered water bottle.

His fingers again stuck to the metal as he took the fuse cord from his gun and cupped it in his fist, blowing on the smouldering end, holding it clear of the splashing water. He was falling behind, tiring more swiftly than the younger man, gasping in the mountain air.

Suddenly he understood why his bullets had flown high: in the thin air their path was flatter. At once he knelt to fire.

This time he aimed lower, whispering, 'My target is big but my bullet is small, my target is big but . . .' His only anxiety was the river water, which might have splashed into his musket barrel and run down to dampen the powder.

'No,' he thought. 'Any water in the barrel will have frozen.'

He saw that this was a deadly danger, but had already squeezed the trigger.

For a while the sergeant lay on his back. Something bad had happened. He touched the side of his face and found its contours unfamiliar. He listened to the stream and to the crows overhead. Very slowly he sat up and leant his shoulder against a rock. Blood dripped from his chin on to the burst gun.

'I have not been shot,' John said aloud, though he was blind with pain. He had been listening for the sergeant's musket, but when it came the sound was so loud and strange that he had fallen. 'I have bruised my head. Nothing more.'

He blundered on, but the boulders were a maze so he turned uphill to give himself direction. Rocks crunched and squeaked underfoot, and he thought that a tiger was gnawing his skull.

He reached the top of the slope, walking more slowly, waiting for the gun's one word, resting against boulders. The shadow lay in the edge of his vision like a black boulder in a stream, and likewise turned him. He was turned or spilled downhill, growing afraid of the mountains, their indifference like hatred, and travelling for an unknown time, though there was at least one freezing night.

He came to a narrow valley. A waterfall hung in rags like Jesus. It was the valley of the monastery and he sat by the pool below the waterfall, watching a stone half covered by the rocking water. Water blinked across the stone like the clear eyelid of a crocodile, and this was so strange that he might have sat there until he died. But his shivering jarred his head. Roused by pain he followed the stream to the tumbledown buildings.

With shelter the pain was worse. He was adopted by the oldest monks, who led him to a cold room where he lay under a blanket that was too short, like every blanket in China, contemplating his feet that were like the feet of a corpse. An old monk slept against his back, reassured by his bulk, and led him by the sleeve to breakfast when he saw the white giant forgetting to eat.

The monks brought lamps to ease his hurt, and he

dedicated their light to his amah, who had certainly brought him here. Indeed, the bullet in his head was the little wooden Buddha from his amah's apron, though he wasn't sure how the sergeant had found it.

He wandered the corridors, sitting down when the fever and chills were bad. He heard nothing from the boy monk, though someone laid a dish of water by his feet, which was a trick mischievous enough for the little imp and against which he was defenceless. Sometimes he thought that the dish was an ink dish, and said, 'My ink is clear water, so I will write about the Buddha.'

Then the monks gave him opium pills and he couldn't move. 'Pain is truth,' he thought, wanting a settlement with the lump of China in his head.

He stopped eating. Ghosts, boneless as water, pestered him at night, and all day the shadow was like a hand on his brow, telling him to stay. He sat on a bench in a corridor, wordless as a holy man, his face turned to the wall, sitting as God sits among His rusty thunderbolts, beaten by China.

He heard rain. Rain clattered on the roof, jetted from gutters, seethed in the yard. It drew him to the side door, where he looked into a haze of rain and saw the swollen stream, which broke over boulders so that its spurtings joined the storm. He couldn't go out because the air was a froth of water in which he might drown and because the stream was like cavalry along the valley, rampant under its flags of foam.

'Terrible as an army with banners,' he thought, and wondered about his wife.

24

At dusk Grace and Jivu Lanu approached a town, but skirted round it on a track through dark fields. They climbed a slope and came to a low hut.

Jivu Lanu pushed her towards the door, which was a sheaf of reeds stuffed into a narrow slit, so low that she entered at a crouch. Inside, an old woman was curled in the gloom on a bed of twigs and bracken. She looked up in alarm, then saw Jivu and opened a toothless grin. She embraced him and spoke a dialect which Grace didn't know.

The old woman laughed as she lit the lamp, then scowled at Grace, who ignored her, staring around the wretched turf hut. 'We'll eat,' said Jivu Lanu. The old woman had two sweet potatoes, roasted on the fire but now cold, and a pot of cold broth.

Without asking, Grace bit into a stale potato then took the watery broth, made of lentils and greens, with mushrooms added from Jivu's pack. She drank deeply until Jivu snatched it away.

The old woman chattered endlessly but ate nothing. She left her bed and curled in a corner of the room, her eyes glinting in the lamplight. She was Jivu Lanu's mother, the former wife of headman Sho. She had reason to fear her son, but now he had returned like a

Yi slavemaster with a prisoner, tall and foreign, who would be sold as a house-slave. At first the foreigner would hobble around her master's house, each wrist tied to its ankle. Then she would be let out, her foot in a great clog, a peg driven in to trap her heel. Her face would be tattooed. She would be made pregnant, again and again until she didn't wish to leave.

When the broth was finished everyone relaxed. Jivu produced rice wine from his pack and the old woman was silent. Sometimes they glanced at Grace, who was staring at some blue glass. It was only a broken piece of bottle on a ledge in the turf wall, but was weirdly luminous. She thought that the Christian Church might try blue glass for its services, then giggled, remembering stained-glass windows.

The old woman had a mask. It was a section of tree bark, black and knotty, with narrow eyeholes and a long snout. Jivu Lanu put it on, tying a ribbon of grubby cloth behind his head.

Grace might have laughed, but she was distracted because she could somehow feel the coils of the knot, as you can feel an ear. She wanted to explain this to Jivu Lanu, but saw only the mask. It was impressive, she decided: perhaps she had underestimated primitive art.

She had been kneeling down but was pushed forward to her hands and knees. The mask and the old woman stared at her. 'This an imposing ceremony,' she thought.

A rug was thrown over her back, but she was thinking how her fingers felt, one against another: she could feel each finger separately, she decided, the sensation not making one event.

Jivu followed her gaze. A pulse of love passed through him because her fingers were like the long fingers of a crocodile. She was his crocodile bride and he moved to lift her skirt.

Grace stopped him, but her wrist was gripped. She relaxed a moment, then twisted free and ran from the house.

Jivu Lanu was bewildered: no crocodile can run on its hind legs. He ran after her. He looked over the dark fields, then stumbled into the night, going where a crocodile would go.

Grace watched stupid Jivu Lanu disappear into the dark. She had run outside, put her foot on a window ledge, and hauled herself to the roof.

She climbed down, pushing aside the old woman, and hurried down the hill, impatient of her blurred senses. She recalled Jivu's fumbling and thought, 'My husband is twice as much a man.' She had taken John's love and would not fear this creature.

The jarring of her steps sent ripples through her body, and she decided she could feel her inner organs. She paused in the darkness because Jivu's broth was a purgative.

She crossed a flat bridge into the town, looking for an inn or the house of the magistrate. But there was a kind of festival: crowds shuffled toe-to-heel, straw hats tipped against straw hats, and she kept stopping to look – once at a lantern, then at a woman's shawl. Food sellers worked under flickering torches. There were fireworks and music. Drunks filled the street, their faces bestial.

Jivu's drug advanced and retreated like a tide, but always renewing with greater force. She drifted with the crowd though her legs wavered under her, part of the liquidization of the world, which was besieged as in the flood of Noah. How fortunate that Jivu had assaulted her too soon: now she would be helpless.

She heard music. Cymbals were like a splash, a gong was whorled as a shell. It was a street theatre. She was carried forward until the actors loomed above her. The play was incomprehensible yet she watched slack-jawed, stupefied by the eternal hopes and suffering of humanity.

The lead actor, in a crimson cloak and gilt headdress, strutted and sang, raging at his soldiers. 'Splendid as Satan,' she thought. She examined the idea that this might be a scene in hell, with the Devil strutting before the damned: she enjoyed this vision, which the potion was helping to make vivid.

The audience seemed to be watching her. She dismissed the notion, wary of her muddled senses. Yet the lead actor was surely addressing her. She was bemused by his headdress, which was trimmed with the tails of foxes and pheasants, and struggled to understand. Did he mean she was distracting his audience? She noticed herself swallow, which meant she was frightened.

The audience looked at her and laughed, and she saw

they were not the captives of hell but its imps and demons. The actor's headdress opened like a flower.

She stepped into an alley. The ground was all flames. She knew that the flames were only orange peel, used as a medicine and here laid out to dry, but it looked like a cellar in hell. Indeed, since she believed in Satan and his works, the potion was showing her the truth.

She wished she hadn't thought of this. The redness flickered on mud walls, which were covered with devil faces: they were only daubed characters, a good-luck slogan, but they jeered at her plainness. She walked on until the alley was utterly dark. She leant her face against a wall and whispered 'Our Father, which art in heaven . . .'

She had to stop because she trembled on the edge of a vision. She heard a treading, which was like the footfall of God: it was only the pulse in her ears, but she was nevertheless awed because the truth is still the truth, by whatever route we find it.

With this thought she was consumed. It was the glory of the hem of the Lord. The folds of His mantle broke over her like a wave. She was a mote in His splendour. He danced at the navel of the world, entranced in Himself. He didn't see her whelmed in his robes, or perhaps He saw but danced on for the furtherance of her understanding. He bestrode worlds, His thunder was imminent, He roped the hurricane.

After aeons, her mind grew again, pushing back the splendour. She was on her knees and stayed there while an age of glory passed away. She rose on cramped legs, helping herself against a wall. The potion was ebbing, and with it her vision, though its force would remain always.

She left the alley. In the dark street a last drunk reeled. The theatre was finished, hunched figures taking down the stage. She felt sick again.

The town was dull and ugly. Perhaps this feeling was due to the potion, but she believed it just. The Chinese were apostates and therefore lived in the desolation of God's absence.

Jeering children followed her. She remembered her childhood on the rim of China and her hopes of changing it. How vain, how vain! China was ancient in evil. She was in the belly of the beast and its nature couldn't hide.

She climbed out of the town and came to the dark of a little orchard. A stone hit her back, then the children vanished. Trees leant about and she heard a stream. She laid her face against a tree, very weary. Perhaps this stream was the last of the river – a starved thing, lost in the mountains sucking stones.

The tree in its crocodile skin was moving under her cheek. She decided to ignore this and lay on her back on the cold ground. Bare branches, crooked as claws, now blocked the sky. A shrivelled apple hung above her, clenched as a boxing glove.

She whispered, 'One must remember that, even ignoring the potion, I am weary from travelling.'

The clenched apple held the scene. The tree had

squeezed it out like an ill. Under the hill's pelt the roots of the tree were spreading. They were gripping like a claw, and she lay stiff on the ground, her fists squeezed, her eyes shut tight against the vision.

'Whatever holds me is also held,' she whispered. She lay in the claw of Satan, but this in turn was enfolded. The Lord had harrowed hell. Relentless love had ploughed the Pit, scattering the imps and cinders.

The ground tipped and levelled under her. In turn, though, it was rocked in God's grace. He was a moving cliff against the legions of hell. His love was stubborn as death and its agents. He noted the fall of a sparrow and would guide His servant. She thought of her vision in the alley, and opposed its glory to this grubby horror.

The potion was weakening. She rolled on her side and vomited. She saw that the grip of Satan had all along been the twisting of her stomach. Her weariness returned and she let the waves cover her.

She slept on the cold ground and was jolted by visions: one showed the serpent in Eden, which at first was the tongue of Satan, and then was a stream, its coils around us still. Even this didn't wake her. Nor was she afraid when the children led Jivu Lanu to her hiding place.

He pulled her out of town on the leather thong. Again they climbed the slope in the dark and came to the hut beside the path.

Grace deserved no consideration, having deceived him. He didn't administer more of the potion before he blew out the lamp and his thin arms clutched her like death. She turned her face away but he bit her ear while the old woman laughed in the dark and clapped.

He was soon satisfied. 'You are nothing compared to my husband,' said Grace, seeing herself as a bridge over this fuss. In recalling John, though, she wounded herself.

She slept, and saw John bestriding mountain tops or, with the side of his hand, redirecting rivers. Twice more she felt Jivu Lanu upon her, and made an accommodation because otherwise it hurt too much.

She thought briefly of her husband, but had fallen too far and didn't wish to be found.

25

Grace and Jivu Lanu were following the edge of a ravine. It was a few paces wide, with sides as steep as an axe-cut, so that they kept well clear and the river was a rustle of hidden water.

They had descended into spring. Plum and wild roses grew in multitudes, their blossoms drifting across the track and into the ravine, so that all morning they walked as to a wedding. She was silent as if defeated, and Jivu didn't use his leather thong. He held its greasy coils as he once held the oiled pigtail of secretary Chang, dragging him backwards through the bushes, his larynx stabbed, his undergarments fouled and the sow following.

Climbing again, they passed among tamarind and banyan, with white and blue rhododendron and scents of pine and fir balsam, the river invisible in its slot. Then the ravine was interrupted. For fifty paces its walls were slumped into a natural basin, perhaps a fallen cavern.

The basin was terraced, and rich with red earth and the green of spring. A strong house of logs stood among the lushness, with smoke from its chimney and a wood-pile outside, the wood thick and straight. A family was bent among the crops of maize, beans and melons. The father straightened to watch them, and his voice boomed in the echoing basin.

Grace and Jivu slithered down the slope of rich earth to the river. Upstream it emerged from the ravine as a waterfall, then crossed the basin in a broad dark pool, where suds of the waterfall rocked on the surface, then surged back between black walls in another roar of broken water.

There was a little ferry. It was only a raft hooked to a rope across the river, but Jivu Lanu noted the ferryman's broad shoulders and the fertile slopes he tended. He thought how the ferry saved the peasants from a drenching, which in the mountains can be fatal, and how such a ferryman might spread himself across the countryside, overcharging passengers, taking scraps of land as payment, making loans, reaching an accommodation with the local warlord and perhaps becoming his lieutenant, perhaps one day supplanting him. With two or three sons, or with a younger brother, he could be a lord in these parts and have many young wives. Then Jivu saw that Grace was gone.

She had stepped on to the raft, wishing to demonstrate Christian fortitude. Jivu was still preoccupied, so she had pulled the traversing rope. Drifting on the deep pool she looked again at the shaman. He was shouting to her, but she could hear nothing above the clatter of the falls.

She had an advantage at last, and dragged the ferry to the middle of the pool. She was too weary to escape: she wanted only to anger Jivu Lanu and be deafened by water.

How good to be free of his talk! She looked at the

waterfall, which was straight as a shelf. She admired the green curve of water at its lip, followed the dropping yellow tresses, stared into the roiling bubbles below. Spray drifted over her and she thought how the children of the ferryman would hear only this incessant rush, which robbed the feeling from a voice, until one day they climbed from the valley and found that voices could be clear.

For the moment they hung like people in a picture. But then the ferryman came, crashing into the pool and cursing in a language she didn't know. Strong and skilful he hauled himself along the rope towards her.

The ferry was five logs bound with bamboo rope tightened with wedges. A bamboo pole stood vertically at one end and was hooked behind the traversing rope. So she lifted the rope off the pole.

The slow current carried her down the pool. Again she noticed a quietness under the roar of the falls, and stared down into green depths where small fishes hung. In the mountains, though, a quiet pool meant only that the river was gathering its strength. Now she could hear the waterfall ahead.

But really she didn't think of much. She lay on the slick tongue of water, with neither means nor will to steer the raft, content to be helpless. The ferryman hung from the rope, his hair plastered over his face, and watched her drift away. His silence said everything: no one could save her from the waterfall.

Jivu Lanu shouted, 'You will die, you will die.'

She wanted to answer, 'But you yourself brought me to a condition where I will risk death,' but would not shout above the noise of falling water.

She had a final lucid thought. They had walked all morning along the lip of the ravine: if she survived the waterfall, Jivu Lanu couldn't reach her from the bank.

But Jivu was pinned against the woodpile, the ferryman's great hands at his throat. He was searched, and a startling quantity of money discovered, as was the leather thong which had fastened Grace. This proved useful when the ferryman climbed into the ravine to find his raft, leaving Jivu bound to a tree, where he was intermittently abused by the ferryman's children.

After an hour the ferryman returned, saying nothing about the raft or the white woman. But he had thought about the money: there was so much that perhaps Jivu should be killed.

For three days Jivu worked without food on the lush terraces around the crossing. At night he was tied with the leather thong to the ferryman's doorpost, amid immovable knots that were cut each morning.

He took his servitude lightly: the ferryman sat above him on the slope all day, a pipe in his mouth, but couldn't guard him for ever. Soon he would be beaten and released. Jivu regretted the loss of Grace's money, though there was relief in once more being a careless wanderer, but he worried about his pack, which was now a toy for the ferryman's children.

The ferryman was thinking about a bridge upriver. It

took much of his trade, but he knew two brothers who could help him destroy it: with Jivu's money he might build his own bridge and charge a toll. But the bridge was a Yunnan bridge – two monstrous chains overlaid with planks. What lie could explain its destruction? Perhaps he would claim that he had repaired it: once in a lifetime a chain rusted through. Or perhaps – and here he refilled his pipe – he would hire sufficient men and simply occupy the bridge. He would let the Miao pass freely, though, for fear of their poison arrows.

Then he found a soldier beside him. It was Yue Fat's sergeant, who sat quietly on the slope, also with a pipe. They swapped glances and the ferryman saw the soldier's torn face. The sergeant went down to Jivu Lanu, then returned to the ferryman. Discussions began.

The sergeant didn't mention that he was alone in these hills, but clearly he was old and unarmed and without authority so far from the Emperor. He only said that Jivu Lanu was a fugitive and should be surrendered to Imperial justice. The ferryman said he understood, but that Jivu was working off a debt. The sergeant answered that of course a reward was payable for Jivu's capture and this could be passed at once to the ferryman.

The ferryman now wondered if he should kill this soldier: Jivu might tell him about the money. But the sergeant stared calmly through his wounds so that nothing happened.

Taking their time, thinking about their reception, Jivu Lanu and the sergeant trekked back to the collector. The sergeant had given all his money to the ferryman, so they slept without blankets under cold, clear skies. The leather thong had been part of the bargain, and at night Jivu Lanu was bound to a tree, or if there were no trees was bent back with his wrists tied to his ankles. Sometimes it was so cold that the sergeant curled against him.

Jivu didn't complain, though he grieved over his pack, confiscated by the ferryman, its contents scattered by his children. He told stories of the earth dragon and the river god, and the sergeant answered with tales of the army. 'It's a great thing to be a soldier,' said Jivu Lanu in his flattering way.

As for secretary Chang and the half-white woman, Jivu sometimes said that they had been killed by bandits, sometimes that they had wandered off in a storm in the mountains, and once that Chang wished to abuse the woman and Jivu had left in disgust. 'Perhaps they are waiting for us with your master,' he might add.

But the sergeant remembered John's story of the murder of secretary Chang, and was glad to have the murderer, and something to tell Yue Fat.

It was late morning when they arrived above the fisher folk village. They watched for an hour from the top of the Hog, but saw only a squad of Imperial troops. They went down to Yue Fat's house, but found it empty.

The sergeant, greatly relieved, took his prisoner down to the beach, where the troops were destroying the empty village of the fisher folk, who had robbed the collector. First they launched the boats into the river, which snatched them away in triumph, at last purging these splinters from its eye. Then they lit the houses, which burned with a satisfying vigour, flaring like torches on their slim stilts until pots and tools fell smoking through the floors.

As they worked, the Imperial troops said that Yue Fat had returned to Canton, his position lost with his household. They were distant with the sergeant, who was tainted by the loss of his men, in return for which he had only one ragged young prisoner and an injury they recognized.

The sergeant said that his soldiers had died heroically in a great battle with bandits, that his gun had burst because he had used stones when their bullets ran out, and that his prisoner was a vicious criminal. But he was suddenly weary and said no more about Jivu's crimes.

That night he deserted. He walked downstream for a month, arriving half-starved at the clan house in his parents' home town, burning his uniform in a corner of the yard and passing on to vanish for ever in the hive of Canton.

The troops left the pebble beach and Jivu Lanu was alone. He searched for loot in the empty houses of Yue Fat and the missionaries, then among the embers of the fisher folk village. He went to Market Village and saw headman Sho in the opium fields, but was driven off by an overseer with a whip.

He spent the night in a half-built house further up the Yi valley, but couldn't sleep because of his triumph: in exorcizing his father's ghost from the pebble beach he had also expelled the lying missionaries, lazy Yue Fat, and those tainted by his father's murder – the headman and the rest of the fisher folk.

In the morning he was woken by builders. Headman Sho was carrying their tools and at once said, 'The white giant murdered my family.'

At midmorning Sho took his brief rest. Jivu had been sitting on the valley side, thinking about the power of his magic, but came down to sit with Sho against the wall of a half-built pig pen.

'Yue Fat was robbed and the fisher folk were blamed,' said Sho, chewing his maize porridge, which he did not share. The aunts – who were guilty, the stinking old whores – had vanished; but Sho – who had done nothing – had been sold by the Imperial troops to the Yi patriarch, whose youngest son was starting this new plantation.

Then this young master arrived. He declared that Jivu Lanu had also lived at the fisher folk village and must likewise be enslaved. Jivu said that he was a Yi, but couldn't recite his ancestry and was disbelieved. He was led to Market Village and whipped to break his spirit, but only thought how he would throw arrows from his eyes to make men sicken or grow well.

He was sent to the fields, but was too inspired to work, so the Yi locked him in the dark until they could sell him into the Cool Mountains. The shackles taught him modesty and he was put to work again. All things flow, he told himself: as during his days with the ferry-master he thought his servitude would be short.

In time he realized his mistake, but by then he had

two daughters by different slave women and a favourite nephew called Tao Yumi, who he was training to be a shaman. He bullied headman Sho, whose *qi* was so reduced that he welcomed slavery, which saved him from women and the river.

Sho grew sick, and Jivu planned a revelation. When Sho was too weak to take revenge, Jivu would tell him about little Shen's death. He would say, 'The child of the murderer was killed by the child of the murdered man.'

By this time a new tax collector had come to the ruined village of the fisher folk. Like secretary Chang he noted the riverport at Market Village. After discussions with the Yi, whose patriarch had lately died and who felt lost amid Imperial politics, the stones of their storehouse were brought by Miao slaves to the beach below the collector's house. The Yi paid for the collector's supervision of their opium: this, and the closure of the riverport, started their long decline.

At the new port, the opium boats no longer had to pay rent for the Yi storehouse, nor – since the collector's soldiers were on hand – to employ a storeman. But their expenses remained surprisingly constant, thanks to a new Imperial duty on their cargoes, payable to the collector and exacted by his soldiers. The soldiers resented these tasks, which were no part of the duties of a collector's bodyguard.

And the collector had forgotten the tribals. They had come to the riverport at Market Village from far upriver and far inland, bringing furs, dried meat, musk, deer horns and the medicinal parts of bears and tigers. They had always disliked the beach with its soldiers and fisher folk, but now squatted perpetually among the pebbles, waiting for the riverboat and afterwards sitting on the headland licking rock salt. At last they reluctantly picked up their bags, now full of tea, incense, salt, sugar and needles, and climbed into the hills in single file, taking a last look at the riverboat that was curved like the eaves of temples: upstream there were only rafts, used as fishing platforms or for crossing streams, though landlords and rich monks sometimes had coracles of yak-hide or planks laid on inflated pigskins and drawn by their retainers, naked in the icy water.

The tribals caused much irritation with their singing and excrement, so the soldiers were required to drive them on to the Hog, though none of the tribes could understand Cantonese nor why they should obey these outnumbered soldiers. It was an endless humiliating task and again the soldiers blamed the collector, who, in this loneliness, was depressed by their anger and dreamt he was trapped on the slithering scree across the river, so high up that no one could hear.

Sensing this weakness, his soldiers drank and gambled. They neglected the task of policing the tribals, who drifted back to the beach, sitting all day with their backs to the collector's house, watching unblinking for the riverboat. They also watched the aunts, who had fled inland and now came back for Yue Fat's money, creeping from the Hog at dawn and rolling back a boulder in the shallows while the tribals stared bewildered at the sodden leather bag kept under stones for the crayfish to nibble. Then the aunts left the river, walking through the mountains for a month, terrified of bandits and the river god they deserted, but arriving safely at a town on the Yangtze.

Here they shared a large house, even after they were married, and became famous for extravagance and a refusal to eat fish, although they owned the best fishing boat with the most handsome young crewmen. They spent their afternoons drinking tea in a bedroom full of clothes, sitting on bolts of unmade cloth, kicking off their shoes and fingering their fine robes with hands that were now soft.

'Strange, strange,' said one of the aunts. She meant that her soft hands were so new that the feel of the clothes seemed to come from her wrists or her nipples or out of the air. She was ignored, and in time the feelings settled on her hands like the old hard skin.

The aunts shared the clothes, but were not mistaken for each other because they were too rich. Besides, the first aunt stayed at home with her servants, the second grew fat, the third went everywhere with a husband she bullied, and the fourth had a son who they all spoiled because he would one day inherit their estate and afterwards tend their spirits.

Jivu Lanu was also content. He grew calm and plump on the Yi plantation and was honoured by the Miao slaves, especially those who had known no other state and were therefore credulous. In turn he was drawn to their animal cults: using the village buffaloes as exemplars he lectured on the flow of food through a digestive tract and of generations through a family, and on how resolve brings success, as his own life proved.

The Yi women came to him during their monthly troubles, so that he was given the lighter work around the house and allowed out with an overseer to search the hills for medicines. He sometimes said, 'Every man must defeat his father,' and even the overseer nodded.

During these wanderings he often looked down at the riverport at the pebble beach, where there were new fisher folk and Chinese traders, and where the collector was now a full magistrate with a garrison. It had been a sump for ill-luck and its wealth was due to him.

One year it was changed by an earthquake, which shook a great fall of scree into the water off the far bank. The river was a little compressed, so that the next flood covered the beach and the headland and swilled down the riverbank, rushing along the road to Market Village where it softened the ground until coffins floated out – especially those of slaves, who were not buried deep. Among them was the headman: he had wished to be buried, against the fisher folk custom, but the river seized him after all, and swept him away.

Thereafter the headland was only a line of rocks into the water, and the river was straighter and deeper, washing away the pebble beach and the still spot where Little Niece had stood. The new fisher folk moved their houses to a strip of shingle next to the bank, so that they were almost land-dwellers.

That was during the age of the warlords. Then came the Miao wars, then the Japanese invaders and finally the Red revolution. Jivu Lanu saw it all, but heard no more about the two white people.

26

Grace had survived the waterfall at the ferry crossing. She had spread herself on the raft and been carried over the falls and swallowed by the splash pool, dragged down interminably as a throat of water worked around her.

She came choking to the surface and crept back onto the raft. Now she drifted where few had gone, down the dank ravine, past tiny untrodden beaches and rocks under cushions of grey-blue moss. Dripping walls of rock rose vertically and ferns met overhead, through which the sun glittered as if through waves. Upsurgings of water made domes in the river.

She thought and felt nothing. The raft bumped and spun along the bank in the irritating way of rafts, but this punishment seemed deserved. A little bird tipped an inquisitive head, fearless in this secret place, its feet half hidden in the moss, its beak yellow with pollen from the vivid flowers it plundered. She stared at the water's inventions.

The ravine grew wider and its sides crumbled. Boulders came to the river in herds and birches made an airy wood up the slopes on either bank, between which she passed like a parade. The river grew shallow and clear over gravel beds where the raft scraped and bumped, jolting her forward.

She was cramped and cold. When the raft grounded on a clay beach she rose on stiff legs, stepping on to a stone as smooth as a tongue and thence ashore. She wandered into the birches and found – as at the pebble beach – that the air was warmer away from the water.

She saw no one all day. She drank at the shaded river and ate something like cress from its slow windings. The river would lead her home, where she would dedicate a solitary life to God. By dusk she had found a bush with a dome of thick foliage that reached to the turf. Inside was bare friable ground, heavy with the scents of earth, where the warmth of the day still lingered. Here she offered up prayers of gratitude for her deliverance. In the morning her clothes were full of blood and her person covered in leeches.

This was the worst of her ordeal in the hills. All day the creatures crept through the lace-holes in her shoes, dripped from trees, hung from her like tongues. She tore them off, but the wounds bled horribly so she let the soft bags of blood fatten until they were satisfied. Dreams of the creatures persisted all her life, but she could balance this horror by recalling her rescue.

She had entered an open space on the valley bottom, trodden bare as if used for a meeting place. Above her on the slope were low huts, round as upturned cups. She sat on a boulder by the river. She was weary and sick and blamed the leeches. She would find an obscure village and toil in silence all her life, alone on the ocean of China.

Then the goitred imbeciles appeared. They streamed

down from the huts, gleeful, their backs as round as their roofs. They were small and hung with rags. Above the sagging bag at their throats, their mouths were lipless slits.

Their eyes hardened. They mewled like whelps and pulled at her clothes. She beat off their hands, but was gripped in a boneless strength. Their assault was like leeches, and under their wordless fumbling her mind began to slip.

But a giant was among them. He swung his great arms.

'Back, damn you,' he cried, in blessed English.

For many years Grace said little about Genesis and Chinese characters. She didn't want to discuss her vision of China as the Lord's betrayer.

After their reunion she had led John back to the pebble beach, that place of disappointment. It was deserted, the village burnt, so they rested for an hour on the veranda of the Mission House, then continued with bitter toil to Market Village, where a riverboat was ready to leave.

John lay on deck in the weak highland sun, its warmth healing his bones, and pointed out the places of his adventure. They transferred to a larger boat in the warm lowlands and he sat all day under an awning, listening to the gossip of the deck coolies and claiming he had once shared their trade, a lie so unlikely that they laughed and were silent.

Grace found the bullet under his scalp. She clipped a

patch of hair and made a slit in the skin, listening to his story about Little Niece and recalling that two of the aunts had likewise been swept downriver. Why had she forgotten this, instead believing the worst?

She squeezed out the slug, squashed and snub-nosed. 'A souvenir?' she said, but John shrank from its squinting face and she dropped it overboard. He disliked the downstream river, which steamed at dawn like a skinned rabbit, then glistened in the sun all day like meat.

By these slow stages they returned to Canton, exhausted and reluctant to speak of their adventures, like the young women that Grace had known as a girl. Here John recovered, going alone through the streets of his boyhood to the Christian cemetery, but avoiding the river where Little Niece might be floating with no face. At the cemetery gates he bought paper houses and boats, and paper money marked 'Bank of Hell', carrying them past the grave of Mr Burkett, who had died only a few months after acquiring Grace and her money.

At the grave of Song Lan, though, John bowed and clapped and made an impressive blaze. She had led him to Grace when at last he had turned towards the shadow instead of away from it, which she had surely intended all along.

John and Grace spent three years among the opium addicts of Canton, then once more took the railway from Haiphong. This time they went to Yunnan-fu, far upriver from the pebble beach, and were one day visited by Miao hunters, escaped slaves of the Yi, who were told of the love of Jesus and returned with their friends until the citizens pulled the roof from the Mission House.

But John and Grace had found their destiny, and built a house among the high valleys of the Miao, who Grace described in her famous book as 'the wretched of the earth and the lowest of the low, slaves to alcohol and lasciviousness, and a prey to self-slaughter, who were joyous at the news that God loved even them, and came in crowds to be baptised'.

In the uplands they were a little removed from the real China and from Grace's vision, which had shown it as a bag of corruption which Providence had sealed against the world. She was glad among the minor races of China, who – it might be argued – were also victims of its colossal Fall.

They raised a second building to house their helpers from Europe and America, with a meeting hall for the thronging Miao converts. Grace hoped their success would spread to the lowlands, whose people might say with the Psalmist, 'I will lift up mine eyes unto the hills, from whence cometh my help.' But the Chinese ignored this cult of slaves, and demanded why – in the Great War convulsing Europe – Christian slaughtered Christian. So Grace and John stayed in the hills, soothing the unquiet China in their blood.

They lived among the headwaters of the great south-eastern rivers of Asia, which lie in adjacent valleys like laced fingers. Yet John conceived a hatred of boats because the sound of water under a hull is like the sound of vomiting, and because he still dreamt about the young soldier in the ropes of the river and Little Niece sporting among silk, a wave her pillow.

Mostly he was too high for rivers, trekking over passes to their scattered parishes, recruiting and supporting native converts, travelling with a band of Miao hunters, spears on his back and a crossbow at his waist, its bolts daubed with deadly nightshade or with venom from the poison sacs of centipedes, which they also hid in bait for tigers. He often glimpsed the mountains towards Tibet, snow-covered even in summer, and remembered the white space on Yue Fat's map, but was content in the foothills thinking how any sportsman would envy his wooden basin and wooden spoon, and the hideous Miao hunting dogs which danced along the trail because their paws were full of worms, and the oatmeal and water for every meal, except when they were lucky in the hunt.

Grace bought him a native rod and line, but he claimed that anglers were notoriously a prey for tigers. Nor did he join the Miao in their search for fish, though it was conducted without boats or tackle: they poisoned streams with the white sap of a vine or, in the dry season, dammed them with rocks and earth, baling out the deepest pools to seize the fish as they burrowed into the mud, though some of the fish had spines and there were beaked turtles.

Usually they hunted deer, and here he was prodigious, his spears outreaching his crossbow bolts, the creature transfixed to the ground until the Miao fell on it with whoops, pinching the plump flanks, eating it at a sitting and rising without a sigh.

At home with Grace he took pencil and paper to describe a Miao hunting party, its methods and equipment. Or perhaps, he thought, he should first discuss how a man freezes at sudden danger while a dog flees, which seemed to reveal the human flaw of too much thought. Or he could say how leeches are removed without breaking off the heads, and how the wound can be staunched with a pinch of red tobacco. Or he could tell how a boar as heavy as himself had fled for three days, until – maddened by spears which dragged along the ground – it raced from a bush and opened his arm to the bone.

The boar would have killed him, except that like the Miao he wore a felt wrap as both cloak and blanket. He wrestled the creature until it was stabbed, then stitched his wounds with needle and thread, then accepted its liver for his part in the hunt. Again he stood in silence while offerings were made to a heathen god. But he didn't feel guilty because all that summer he had pondered a new synthesis in which the Buddha sat at the right hand of God to show that when God had divided the One, separating light from darkness and land from sea, He had also separated good from evil and was thus the Lord of both. But John found no place in this synthesis for China's godlings and whiskered demons and his vision therefore faded.

At last, with many sighs and crossings-out, he wrote: *It is less difficult than might be thought to accustom oneself to going barefoot, except for the thorns. Hunters should remember, however, that bare heels are noisy when travelling swiftly over hard, hollow ground.* But then his pencil faltered and his head sank towards the lines, which wavered like water. Grace watched him nodding lower and lower until he woke with a snore, but didn't help.

She rarely thought of her time with the fisher folk, or of her journey with Jivu Lanu, which had frightened her less than John's recent adventure with the Yi landlords: they had hung him for two days from a roof beam, shouting *'Ta t'a! Ta t'a!'* – 'Beat him! Beat him!' – and cursing Christianity because it taught the Miao that they mattered. They demanded a ransom of silver bars, then started towards the Cool Mountains, where he would have lived and died in servitude had he not been rescued by his comrades from the hunting party.

She had hoped to find relics of Israel in the high shrines of the region or the speech of its peoples, but found only stories of a flood to lay with the story of Noah, although these local floods were brought by a river. One winter she made a script for the Miao, who had no written language. She derived it from their own culture, so that the character for 'skirt' used a shape from their embroidered hems, and 'river' was like the hook-shaped bend in a river near their house, though this perhaps was too different from rivers elsewhere. Her Miao friends received her script with courtesy, though its success became doubtful after every missionary was swept from China in another great convulsion.

They worked thereafter in a wooden meeting hall in a suburb of Philadelphia, where Grace preached in a nervous murmur. Her sermons were full of tortured thought, and the congregation of old ladies stared instead at John, who sat in noble profile near his wife, with wild white hair like a prophet from the desert.

Other locals were indifferent like the Chinese, but less persuaded by tea and a warm stove. Grace saw that China was not alone in abandoning the Father, and remembered when she had first learned that there were sinners even in Christendom.

In the city library she sought other links between China and Israel, drawing genealogies of the sons of Noah or bending over maps to trace their likely path through the mountains, where the blue roots of the river were like the veins under your tongue. One book said that the river was older than the mountains, which were rising with the Himalayas, but of course this was absurd, as she explained to John, since without mountains the river couldn't flow.

John thought of the river before Genesis, flowing through a desert of devils. He never argued about religion, however, because he wouldn't hurt Grace again and because he remembered the bullet in his head: he had floated in the river while the gods of China rose to seize him, and in the monastery he had been so cold.

In Philadelphia they were remote from promotion within the Mission, and anyway couldn't compete with the veterans of Africa and South America. They were too old to return to China, even during its brief times of peace, and unpacked their last camphor-wood trunk. Their apartment above the meeting hall – two stark rooms that were icy on winter mornings and suffocating in summer – filled with the smells of China.

Now, in an old unposted letter, she found mention of her discoveries of Genesis in Chinese characters. She thought of her lost journal, filled with such researches but thrown into the river by Jivu Lanu: perhaps the fisher folk had caught it downstream, though its words would be dissolved. But she remembered all her discoveries and wrote them into a proper essay, though the characters seemed like little nets which catch the fish but not the river.

'Away with words,' she thought, a little surprised because her jokes were nowadays rare.

Still, thinking that the work might be lost, she sent her essay to the Mission's headquarters in New York. She received a courteous acknowledgement but nothing further. Finding herself there on other business, she sought out the head of the China section.

He was startlingly young. She addressed him in Mandarin then Cantonese. Without embarrassment he said he would rather speak English. She had no idea that the mission to China had sunk so low, and took a moment to collect herself. Nevertheless he gave permission for her work to be published, though of course at her own expense. As he shook hands he praised her researches as 'really ingenious', which was not what she desired.

Grace didn't cease her contacts with the Chinese, whose grief continued as it had for millennia, and would only end when they turned to the Lord and to the Western ways which would bring them primacy in the world. She was consoled by her grandsons, so eager to help China from its blindness, and recalled that the Lord forgave even apostasy, saying, 'If from thence thou shalt seek the Lord thy God, thou shalt find him. He will not forsake thee.'

Indeed, Grace and John had proved fruitful, their first child being born in the year following her ordeal with Jivu Lanu. This girl was the most Chinese of their children. In her thirties she abruptly moved to New York and married the elderly owner of a restaurant in Chinatown, who was not a Christian. Even in that community she was taken for a full-blooded Chinese, which was strange since her inheritance was only a quarter Oriental.

But Grace and John did not consider such things, since every child is sent from the Father and equally deserves our love.

BIBLIOGRAPHY

Many works contributed to this book, some supplying only a single fact: the incision which kills secretary Chang, for instance, is explained in Zheng Yi's *Scarlet Memorial*, and Yue Fat's map originated in *The River at the Centre of the World* by Simon Winchester.

But the major sources are as follows:

The Age of Wild Ghosts, by Erik Mueggler (University of California Press, 2001). As well as explaining the life-cycle of hungry ghosts and supplying Jivu Lanu's exorcism chant, this book inspired the ideas of female pollution so eagerly espoused by headman Sho. Remarkably, Dr Mueggler's observations in the highlands of south-west China were made as recently as the 1990s.

The Discovery of Genesis, by C. H. Kang & Ethel Nelson (Concordia, 1979)

A'Chu, by Emma T. Anderson (Review & Herald, 1920)

In the Eyes of the East, by Marjorie Barstow Greenbie (Dodd, Mead, 1921)

Travels in Imperial China, by George Bishop (Cassell, 1990)

Kwang Tung, or Five Years in South China, by J. A. Turner (S. W. Partridge, 1894)

The Junkman Smiles, by G. R. G. Worcester (Chatto & Windus, 1959)

The Tourist's Guide to Canton, the West River and Macao (Noronha, 1895)

Three Weeks on the West River of Canton, by Revd Dr Legge, Dr Palmer and Mr Tsang Kwei-Hwan, etc. (Hong Kong, 1866)

Slaves of the Cool Mountains, by Alan Winnington (Lawrence & Wishart, 1959)

Among those who read this book in manuscript I'm particularly grateful to Maria Rejt, Christopher Wakling, Professor Erik Mueggler of the University of Michigan, and Professor Morris Rossabi of Columbia University, New York.